Chasing Paper

Part 2

By: Marlin Ousley

First print 2019 September

This is a book of fiction. Any references or similarities to actual events, real people, or real locations are intended to give the novel a sense of reality. Any similarity to other names, characters, places and incidents are entirely coincidental.

ISBN-13: 9781697222371

Cover Design: Crystell Publications

Book Productions: Crystell Publications
You're The Publisher, We're Your Legs
We Help You Self Publish Your Book
(405) 414-3991

Printed in the USA

ACKNOWLEDGEMENTS

With every new book, writing acknowledgements becomes harder because I'm afraid that I'll leave someone important out, so if for some reason you do not see your name, please forgive me.

God is still number one because without his blessings, none of this would be possible.

To my parents, Joyce Ousley and Willie Ousley (R.I.P.), thanks for instilling in me a never quit attitude. I'm sure it's not easy accepting that your son writes streets lit, but your support for me never wavered. I appreciate it and both of you.

To my kids, I love you more than words can say. The joy y'all bring to my life can never be measured. To my son Lil Marlin, I'm proud to call you mine, but it's not easy to walk in my shoes (smile). To my son Anthony, I'm your biggest supporter, but never forget that I love you, more than the streets do. To my daughter Alexadra, the love I have for you inspires me to continue no matter how hard it gets.

To my family, Marlina, Audrey, Marvel, Tiara, Trellaine, Bobo (R.I.P.), Maya, Haps, J-Bo, Dj, Mark, Lil Willis, Marleane, Marvin, David, Karen, Bob, Gene, Aunt Cecile, Emani, Emari, Lil Marlin III, Maraya, Mizani, Antonae, Nathan, Tara, Rocko, Noah, Misline, Cameron, Clarissa Pooh, Anthony (R.I.P.), Tayla, Boobie, and all those I'm close to from Jacksonville, FL., Panama City, FL., Pensicola, FL., Palm Beach, FL., Troy, Alabama, Montgomery, Alabama, California, and Chicago. Thanks for the love and support.

To my friends and supporters, black Rick (true friendship can never be measured in words), Lori Davis (I'm truly thankful for you and all the help you've given me), Tamela Burgess (you are a godsend), Ardena Burroughs, let's take flight I'm waiting on that book from you (smile), Cheryl Brimberry (I'll always be in debt to you), to everyone from the neighborhood who purchased my books, I truly appreciate the support and I promise to keep putting out hits.

To Crystell Publication for all your help and insight. I thank you for putting up with my countless letters and inquiries. You are truly a blessing.

To those who befriended me then tried to stab me in the back, I ain't mad at you cause you can't knock the hustle.

Thanks to all the people who spread the word about my books, thanks to the thousands of people who wish me well and tell me to keep my head up. When I get home, I'm throwing a big ass part and everyone's invited (lol).

To the lovely ladies from South Bay, Belle Glade, Pahokee, Clewiston, and Palm Beach (You know who you are). I may not say much but I fucks with y'all and when I get out of here, I'm coming through to holla at y'all (Real Talk).

To my fans for your continued support I sincerely thank you.

To those who told me I couldn't do it, do you believe me now?

To Avery, Q, Amp, Pep, Beiro, Bayer, Clark, Freddy Brit, Shanky Boy, Bird, Mingo, Ty, Zavi, Pitch Black, Head, Trav, Terrio, Terrance Green, Wayne, Twin, Soldier, Al,

Twan, Monday, Mel, 305, Kareem, Green, Billy, Papa Zoe, Eric, Willie Hunter, Lil One, Scooter, Mike, Joe, Red Rick, Twan, Jack, Celo, A.K., Haition, Nip, Willie, Flaco, Ira Bunion (We gone do big things together), and everyone else who has read my books and given me their honest opinion. Believe it or not, y'all keep me on point. Circle Six Publishing is in the building, now watch me kick the door down (Lol).

If I've forgotten anyone, don't take it personally. Either I've honestly forgotten you or I don't fuck with you at all.

Now sit back, relax, and enjoy 'cause this shit's so real you'll think you lived it.

Recap from Part 1

CHAPTER 26

"Alright, everybody, quiet down!" Detective Nelson screamed as he stood behind the podium in the packed squad room, and after the room quieted down, he picked his words carefully.

"Now could somebody explain to me how our two suspects managed to escape in spite of a heavily guarded perimeter, K-9 Units, and a chopper in the air?"

"We don't know, sir," someone answered.

"Who said that?"

"I did," the officer said.

"Stand up, please. Now, what's your name?"

"Rogers, sir."

"Okay, Officer Rogers, now you just said that you didn't know but let me show you why I can't accept that answer. I just left the widows of those slain officers and five children who lost their fathers. They don't want to hear that we don't know what happened to them. Instead, they want answers and quite frankly, so do I."

"Uh, detective, they might've gotten lucky and got away but we may have learned something that could be useful in catching them," another officer said.

"Alright, let's hear it."

"Well, while interviewing several of the homeowners, we've learned that a maroon colored four door Toyota Camry was seen in the area around the same time. We checked with the other homeowners in the area and none of them owns a car fitting that description. However, we went back, viewed the surveillance tapes from the bank's parking lot and the car can be seen leaving shortly after the suspect fled."

"You think they could've been accomplices?"

"It's a possibility, but in my opinion, no, because then how would you explain the suspect's getaway car being left in the parking lot?"

"Hmm! Good point."

"Now, we do view the scene from inside the bank during the robbery and it clearly shows one of the suspects walking over to where two African American females lay."

"You think it's possible that they knew each other?"

"Well, it's unclear if any words were exchanged between them but it's definitely a possibility. The same two women can be seen on the surveillance tape running out of the bank and driving away in a red or maroon Toyota Camry."

"Alright, so let's get this straight. During the robbery, one of the suspects walks over to where two African American females are laying but it's unknown if any words were exchanged between them?"

"That's correct."

"Then, after our suspects flee, these same two women are seen running out of the bank and driving away in the same car that some of the homeowners claim they saw in the area where the suspects were last seen?"

"Right again, sir."

"Well, have these women been identified?"

"No, sir."

"And why not?"

"Well, we're running a facial recognition program as we speak and we're also checking the NCIS System. As for the car, there was no tag. Instead, there was a temporary tag in the back window and from the surveillance footage, it's impossible to read it."

"Alright, well here's what I want to do," Detective Nelson said. "The first think is I want to look at myself is the surveillance tape. Just maybe something went unnoticed and a fresh pair of eyes will spot it. Then, I want a copy of the tape sent to the feds for analysis. They have more sophisticated equipment than we do and they just might be able to get a read on that temporary tag. Ladies and gentlemen, we have two cop killers on the loose and I want them caught. You've also heard about the two African American females from the bank who were seen in the area where the suspects were last seen. Identify and find them. You may even want to enlist the public's help. Either way, we need to get these animals off the streets. Now, let's get it done, people. Time's a wasting." Detective Nelson said as the room began clearing out, and after quickly grabbing his briefcase, he headed for his office. A short time later, an officer arrived with a copy of the tape and after signing for it, he inserted it into the machine. Then after pulling up a chair, he grabbed the remote and pressed play.

***

"Oh, so what, you're tired?" Tamaya asked jokingly.

"Nah, I'm just tryin to give you a break," Curt replied with a smirk.

"Mmm hmm! Like I told you, if you get it up, I'll put it down."

"Alright, just give me a minute."

"Yeah, alright, but have you figured out what you gon do?"

"About what?"

"You know, about the police looking for you and Snag."

"Ain't too much I can do. I mean, cause no matter what, they ain't gon stop looking for us."

"I know, but don't you think y'all should at least go somewhere?"

"Go where?"

"I don't know, but anywhere other than here will do."

"You need money to go on the run."

"Well, y'all got money."

"A hundred thousand dollars ain't no money, especially when you're running for your life."

"What about the money from the other robbery?"

"It still won't be enough. I mean, once we leave, we can't never come back and that means we need a lot more money."

"What if I helped you get the money?"

"And how you plan to do that? Wait a minute! If you're thinking what I think you're thinking, hell, nah!"

"Why, cause I'm a girl?"

"That too, but I'm not getting you involved in my shit."

“Nigga, I’m already involved. I’m the one who picked y’all up, remember?”

“Yeah, but that ain’t the same as going up in a bank. What if something happens and you have to shoot somebody?”

“Then I’ll shoot ‘em,” she replied nonchalantly.

“Girl, you crazy!”

“Oh, but I wasn’t crazy when I put y’all ass in my damn trunk?”

“That was different.”

“How? ‘Cause if them crackas would’ve caught us, I would be in jail right now along with y’all ass.”

“Alright, but why would you even want to do that?”

“Cause for one, I could use the money, and two, I don’t want to see you go to jail. If that happens, all this will go to waste,” she said as she began fondling him.

“That shit ain’t easy like everybody thinks.”

“Well, you could show me what to do,” she replied while massaging him back and forth. After he’d become fully aroused, she climbed up and straddled him.

“I tell you what. Let me think about it.”

“Alright, but I’m serious.”

“Me too,” he shot back while gently massaging her ass, and as he looked up at her lustfully, she positioned him at her opening before lowering herself and taking him all the way inside of her.

Meanwhile, downstairs, Snag was just going through the motions as he slid his dick in and out of Crystal. On his mind, instead, was the fact that they’d killed two police officers, and with the police scouring the city looking for them, he was seriously contemplating what to do next.

Crystal knew that he had a lot on his mind. Who wouldn't after all that had happened. Wanting to take his mind off the situation if only for a little while, she'd coaxed him into bed, and sensing that it wasn't working, she decided to try something different.

Suddenly pushing him up off of her and onto his back, she climbed up on her hands and knees before leaning down to kiss him passionately.

Then, as he looked up at her with a surprised look on his face, she kissed a trail down to his stomach while gently massaging his dick. After licking the underside and teasing the head, she took him in her mouth and as she began sucking him in and out of her throat, he threw his head back and closed his eyes. Damn! He said to himself as she deepthroated him over and over, and as the tension began to build, he tried to stay focused. Increasing her pace, Crystal licked and sucked him with abandon, and minutes later, it all payed off as he came, flooding her mouth with his seed.

"Mmm!" She moaned while swallowing his load and satisfied with her performance, she looked up at him.

"Feel better now?"

"Yeah, but I'm still tryin to figure out how shit got so fucked up. I mean, two police got killed and now them ma'fuckers ain't gon stop looking till they find us."

"Look, let's just get some sleep and when we wake up, we can figure out what we gon do."

"Yeah, alright," he replied while pulling her close and while dozing off to sleep, he thought about the situation he'd gotten himself into and knew that there would be no easy way out of it.

CHAPTER 27

"Damn! Look at all the ass on that bitch right there," Ray Ray screamed as they walked into the King of Diamonds strip club located on 178th and Northeast 5th Avenue.

"Yeah, and you thought the ho's we had at the house were bad."

"Man, they ain't got shit on these ma'fuckers up in here. Look at that thick red bone right there."

"Damn, man. Just chill and stop acting like you ain't never been nowhere," Trigga said as they searched for somewhere to sit, and suddenly spotting an empty table across the room, they both headed for it. After reaching the table and taking a seat, they stared in awe at all the scantily clad women walking around. A short time later, a waitress approached them.

"Good evening, would you gentlemen like to order something to drink?"

"Yeah, bring us a bottle of Grey Goose and some cranberry juice," Trigga said. "Oh, and can I get twenty five hundred dollars in ones please?"

"Of course, just give me a minute." The waitress replied before walking off, and suddenly pulling a wad of cash out of his pocket, he quickly counted out thirty one hundred dollar bills before settling back in his chair.

"Excuse me, would y'all like a dance?" Someone suddenly asked, and looking up, they came face to face with one of the prettiest women they'd ever seen. Standing five feet four inches tall, and weighing a hundred and thirty five pounds, the caramel colored beauty was thick in all the right places and with her piercing green eyes, there was no way they were going to tell her *no*.

"Hell, yeah!" Ray Ray screamed while looking her up and down and as "Welcome to My Hood" by D.J. Khaled began blasting from the speakers, she turned around and dropped it like it was hot.

Damn! They both said to themselves while watching her ass bounce up and down and just when they thought it couldn't get any better, she removed her top before shaking her 36 DD's in their face. Then after removing the bottom half, she bent over in front of them, grabbed both ass cheeks, and spread 'em giving them a bird's eye view of her neatly trimmed pussy. Slapping her on the ass in amazement as she performed for them, and mesmerized by her voluptuous body, he didn't see the waitress approaching until she was standing next to them.

"Here's your drink," she said while setting the bottle inside a bucket of ice on the table.

"How much I owe you?" Trigga asked.

"One fifty."

"Alright, here," he said before handing her two one

hundred dollar bills and as she attempted to give him the change, he told her to keep it.

"Thanks, sweetie," she replied before pulling out a pouch and unzipping it. Then removing twenty five separate stacks of a hundred ones, she placed them on the table. Smiling devilishly, Trigga counted out twenty five one hundred dollar bills before handing them to her and patting her on the ass before she walked off. He turned and handed the remaining hundred dollar bill to a dancer walking by.

Noticing the stack of money on the table, several dancers approached them and after turning most of them away, Ray Ray finally chose a dark skinned dancer with a big butt. As the two dancers danced their hearts out, Trigga and Ray Ray sat back and enjoyed the show, and taking a sip of their drinks, they smiled while imagining what else the night had in store.

***

"Hey, Chambers!"

"Yes, sir."

"Come here for a minute," Detective Nelson said after stepping out into the hall.

"What's going on, detective?" Officer Chambers asked walking up.

"I've got something I want you to take a look at. I've looked at the surveillance tape from the bank robbery at least ten times and something just keeps jumping out at me, but I need to know if it's just me or if somebody else sees what I see."

"Alright, well let's see what you're talking about," Officer Chambers said before stepping into the room.

"Well, you really don't have to view the whole thing, just a segment of it, but when you do, tell me the first thing that comes to mind."

"Alright, I got you," Officer Chambers replied and after pulling up a chair, he watched as Detective Nelson pressed play on the remote control. Suddenly, a grainy black and white image of inside the bank appeared on the screen and after several intense minutes, two men wearing ski masks and carrying automatic weapons rushed inside before disarming the security guard and ordering everyone to the floor. While one of the suspects stood watch, the other one addressed the bank's patrons, but without audio, it was impossible to tell what he was saying.

Suddenly walking over to the tellers, the suspect said something to them before handing them a bag and as they began emptying their drawers into it, the other suspect spotted what looked like words being exchanged between two African American females and rushed over to them. Now standing over them, it's obvious he said something because as one of the women looked up at him, he paused momentarily.

"Right there!" Officer Chambers screamed.

"What did you see?"

"I'm not sure, but play it again," he said as Detective Nelson rewinded the tape, and after pressing play, Officer Chambers leaned forward in his chair while keeping his eyes glued to the screen.

"Now when I tell you to hit pause, okay?"

"Okay," Detective Nelson replied while keeping his hand on the button and suddenly, without warning, Officer Chambers gave the word.

"Now!"

"Alright, what do you see?" Detective Nelson asked while watching him closely.

"Right here, it's like her eyes are saying I know this person."

"So it's not just me."

"What?"

"Nothing, I was just saying that I thought the same thing when I saw it. You know how you see someone you know, but it kind of catches you by surprise?"

"Yeah."

"Well, that's what her expression is saying to me. Sort of like *hey, I know you*."

"Right, and if you pay attention, you can see him hesitate as soon as she looks up at him."

"So, now, let's rethink this," Detective Nelson said before turning to face Officer Chambers. "Our two suspects run out of the bank only to find a police car parked behind their getaway car. So what do they do? After shooting the two officers, they fled on foot."

"Then what?"

"Well, according to the surveillance tape, both women got up and ran out of the bank before jumping into their car and driving off. Now suppose the two women do know our suspects. Maybe they saw them running and decided to pick 'em up."

"It's plausible, but why involve yourself in something of

this magnitude? I mean, they just killed two police officers for God's sake."

"Yeah, but who knows why some people do the things they do."

"All I know is that from what I see, there's a possibility that those two women know our suspects and if they assisted them in any way whatsoever, they're going to jail for accessory after the fact, aiding and abetting, and whatever else I can think of," Detective Nelson replied.

"Alright, so the key is the two women from the bank?"

"My hunch tells me you're correct. It also tells me that if we find them, we find our suspects."

"Alright, now all we have to do is find them," Officer Chambers said as he stood up to leave, and after opening the door, he stepped out into the hall with the detective on his heels.

"Make sure you keep me informed about what's going on."

"Will do," Officer Chambers said before walking off and after walking back into his office and closing the door behind him, Detective Nelson took a seat and stared up at the face on the screen.

Now
Part 2 Begins ….

CHAPTER 28

"Hey, Tamaya, wake up!"

"Huh."

"Wake up."

"Boy what?" She said groggily while rolling over to face him.

"Were you serious about what you said earlier?"

"What I said about what?"

"You know, bout you wanting to help me rob a bank."

"Yeah, I was serious." She replied while rubbing the sleep from her eyes, "But you woke me up to ask me that?"

"Nah, I woke you up to tell you that if you're serious, we can do it."

"Ohh, for real!"

"Yeah, but you gon have to do exactly what I tell you to do cause if this ain't done right, we're dead."

"Alright," Tamaya said while tryin to contain her excitement and suddenly thinking about the money she could get, she wanted to get out of bed and jump for joy.

"Now, the first think you gon need to do is learn what

your role's gonna be."

"Alright, so we gon talk about it in the morning, right?"

"Nah, we gon talk about it right now."

"Boy, it's two o'clock in the morning."

"So? We can sleep after we get this money," he replied before grabbing the AK from the side of the bed.

"Boy, what you doin with that?"

"This is the gun you'll be using so I gotta make sure you know how to use it."

"Now?"

"Yeah, so come on."

"Alright," she said throwing the covers off of her. "Can I at least get dressed first."

"Yeah, hurry up."

"Okay," she replied before grabbing a pair of her panties out of her drawer and stepping into them. Then, after slipping on a t-shirt, she walked over to him.

"You ever shot one of these?"

"Yeah, I got one in the closet."

"Look, I'm serious."

"Boy, you know I ain't never shot one of these."

"Well, it ain't hard, so listen up. You see this right here?"

"Yeah."

"This is the trigger and it shoots every time you pull it. You see this lil switch right here?"

"Yeah."

"That's the safety, if you flip it like this, it won't shoot, but if you flip it like this, it will. You got it?"

"Yeah, I got it."

"Alright, now you see this little button right here? That

releases the clip."

"What's a clip?"

"This right here."

"And what does it do?"

"It holds the bullets."

"Oh."

"Now, if you push it, the clip comes out like this," he said demonstrating. Most likely, you won't have to worry about it. But I'm showing you just so you'll know."

"Alright," she said paying attention.

"You got all that so far?"

"Yeah."

"Alright, here, take it."

"What?"

"I said take it, you're gonna be using it so you might as well get use to holding it."

"Alright, now what?"

"Now, I want you to hold it so that you're comfortable."

"But it's so big."

"You ain't complain about holding something else that was big."

"You know what I mean," she said with a smirk.

"Yeah, alright, now check it. When we go in the bank, I'm gon yell for everybody to get on the floor. At the same time, I'll take care of the security guard, but while I'm doing that, I'm gon need for you to keep an eye on everybody else. Think you can do that?"

"Yeah."

"Okay, and once I get the security guard on the floor, I'll have the tellers put the money in the bag."

"Alright, but suppose somebody tries something?"

"You do whatever you have to do to change their mind. Remember what I did when I saw you and Crystal talking?"

"Yeah, and what would you have done if it wasn't us?"

"Trust me, you don't want to know," Curt replied. "Anyway, nine times out of ten, once they see that we ain't playin, we won't have no problems. Now once we get the money, we get out of there as fast as possible."

"Well, it sounds simple."

"It is if you know what you're doing."

"Well, let's make sure that that ain't gon be no problem."

"Alright, so how does it feel?"

"It alright, I mean how is it supposed to feel?"

"No way in particular, just whatever makes you feel comfortable."

"Okay," she said while adjusting the gun in her hands.

"Now where's the trigger?" he asked suddenly.

"Right here."

"Alright, what's this?"

"The clip, right?"

"Yeah, and what goes in it?"

"Bullets."

"Alright, so far so good," he said smiling. "What's this little button?"

"It releases the clip."

"What about this little thing?"

"That's the safety."

"Good, now the next thing we gon practice is how we gon turn up in the bank. We gon act like the room is the bank so we gon go out in the hall and rush in," he said while heading for the door, and after opening it and stepping out in the hallway, Tamaya came out right on his heels.

"You remember what I said we were gon do when we went in?"

"Yeah, you said you was gon yell for everybody to get on the floor, and at the same time, you was gon take care of the security guard."

"Alright, and what are you gon be doing?"

"Keeping my eye on everybody else to make sure they don't try nothing."

"That's right," Curt said smiling. "Now I'll rush in first and you come in right behind me. Whichever way I go, you go in the opposite direction. That way, we'll have everybody covered."

"Alright, but let me ask you a question. While you're over there dealing with the tellers, is there any place in particular that I'm supposed to stand?"

"Not really, but it's good to be by the door just in case somebody comes in. Plus, you'll be in a position to see the whole bank."

"Oh, okay."

"Now, when we go in, I'll order everybody on the floor while dealing with the security guard. What's your job?"

"To watch everybody and make sure they don't try nothing."

"Right, now you ready?"

"Yeah."

"Alright, let's go," he said before rushing into the room, and suddenly veering to his right, he watched as Tamaya went left. Smiling to himself, he turned toward her and the sight of her standing there in a t-shirt and panties holding an AK seemed rather amusing.

"What?"

"Nothing, I'm just looking at you."

"Alright, so how did I do?"

"You did good, but let's do it again," he replied, and as they headed back into the hallway, he was impressed with her ability to grasp things so quickly. But knowing what was at stake, he thought back to the old adage, practice make perfect.

***

"So, what's up, you coming home with me?" Trigga asked while sitting with the big booty caramel colored dancer.

"Boy, I done told you what time it is."

"Yeah, and I told you I got you."

"Mmm hmm! I hear you talkin."

"Look, I ain't one of these niggas who be..." Trigga said before reaching into his pocket to pull out a wad of cash. "If I say I got you, then that's what it is."

"Alright, just let me go grab my stuff," the dancer replied before walking off, and while watching her ass jiggle, somebody suddenly approached their table.

"Damn, I see y'all boys up in here chillin, huh?" The man named Chris said.

"Yeah, a nigga just chillin," Ray Ray replied.

"Well, I saw y'all boys over here so I came by to holla."

"Yeah, I feel you. Hey, you still doin your thang in Opa-

Locka?" Trigga asked suddenly.

"Yeah, why what's up?"

"Nothing, but check it. How much you be getting them thangs for?"

"Bout twenty six for a whole one, and thirteen for a half. What, y'all boys thinking bout copping some work?"

"Nah, but I can give you a good deal on some."

"On some what?"

"Some work."

"Hold up! So y'all—"

"Look, I got a brick and a half," Trigga said cutting him off, "And all I want for it is thirty stacks."

"Are you serious?"

"Hell, yeah I'm serious, and it's top of the line."

"Alright, can I at least see it?"

"Yeah, it's in my car."

"Alright, but I don't have thirty grand on me."

"How much you got?"

"Bout fifteen, and I can give you ten now and twenty more in the morning."

"Man, a nigga ain't—"

"Damn nigga, y'all know my moneys good." Chris said cutting him off. "I mean, even if I gave you the whole fifteen tonight, you still can't get the other fifteen til in the morning."

"Alright, but man, don't let me have to come looking for you."

"Nigga, you know better than that. I don't hide from nobody. Just come by in the morning and I got you."

"Alright, well, I'm waiting on the lil baby. When she

comes out, I'll be ready to go," Trigga said, and as soon as the words left his mouth, the green eyed beauty walked up.

"You ready?"

"Yeah, come on," Trigga said before heading for the door, and with Ray Ray and Chris right on his heels, he made his way to the car.

Finally reaching it, he opened the door to let the young lady in. Then after walking to the back of the car, he opened the trunk and removed a black bag.

"Here," he said handing the bag to Chris.

"Damn, y'all ridin with this shit in the trunk?" he replied while unzipping the bag, and as soon as the aroma reached his nose, he knew...

"Damn, y'all can't get no more this shit?"

"If we do, we'll holla at you."

"Alright then, get at me in the morning."

"Yeah, alright," Trigga said before closing the trunk, and after watching Chris hurry off, Trigga and Ray Ray climbed in the car, started it up, and drove off.

Meanwhile, they never payed attention to the car that pulled out after them.

CHAPTER 29

"Alright, now what?" Craig asked while following them out onto 441.

"We follow 'em and see where they go," Blue replied.

"See where they go! Man, them ma'fuckers giving our money away to them ho's in the strip club and I'll bet you that the bag he gave that other nigga had our shit in it."

"Okay, but I know him."

"What!"

"The nigga who they gave the bag to. His name is Chris. He be trappin out there in Opa-Locka."

"Alright, but how is that gon get us our shit back?"

"Look, tomorrow I'll go holla at him and explain to him what happened."

"Alright, but suppose he ain't tryin to hear it?"

"Then I'll have to persuade him another way."

"How?"

"Don't worry about it, just keep your eyes on the road and watch them niggas up there."

"Oh, I got them," Craig replied as he followed the car through the Golden Glades Interchange and out onto 7th Avenue.

"I'll bet they're headed back to the Diamonds."

"Probably, but they got one of those stripper ho's with 'em so they could be going to a hotel." Blue said while contemplating their next move and as the car up ahead came to a stop at the light on 151st street and 7th Avenue, Craig did the same three cars back.

"So you figured out how we gon' handle this?" Craig asked while waiting for the light to turn green.

"Oh, I know exactly how we gon handle it," Blue replied. "The only thing I'm trying to figure now is where and when."

"Shit, but that's how ma'fuckas make mistakes. You see, most niggas run off their emotions but if a nigga wants to last out here, he's got to think before he acts. First you do your homework, then you plan, and finally you execute the plan. When it's all said and done, not only will you have handled your business, but you'll stay out of jail, too."

"Damn nigga, since when you started getting all philosophical and shit?"

"Since I realized that jail ain't for me," Blue replied. "I mean, it don't bother some niggas but I hate that shit."

"Yeah, I feel you, cause I hate it, too."

"So that means we gotta be smart. Now, these niggas ridin round like shit's gravy, but trust me, by the time they realize different, it's gon be too late."

Suddenly the light changed, and as the cars began moving, Craig kept the car up ahead in sight as they traveled down 7th Avenue.

After finally approaching the diamonds, they watched as Trigga turned up into the parking lot and parked, and to keep from being seen, Craig kept going while "Bushes" by Plies played out the speakers.

***

"What's wrong?" Crystal asked after rolling over and seeing Snag laying there staring up at the ceiling.

"I can't sleep," Snag replied.

"I can see that, but something else is on your mind."

"Yeah, I'm trying to figure out what I'm going to do. I mean, two police got killed and if them crackas catch me, they gon bury my under the jail."

"So that means we gon have to make sure you don't get caught."

"Yeah, but at the same time, I can't just hide here in the apartments."

"So where you gon go?"

"I don't know, but I'm gon have to go somewhere."

"Maybe, but then again maybe not."

"What you mean?"

"What I mean is the police don't know who y'all are, right?"

"No, not yet, but who knows how long that's gon last."

"Have you talked to Curt?"

"Yeah, but he act like shit's all good. I talked to him about sittin on the money and not drawing attention to ourselves, and the nigga had the nerve to tell me that he wants to buy a Cadillac Escalade."

"Everybody's buying those, so it won't seem to out of the ordinary."

"True, but everybody ain't using money they got from robbing a bank."

"Well, I can't argue with you on that," Crystal said. "I just wish you didn't have to leave."

"Yeah, me too, but what other choice I got? I mean, robbing the bank was bad enough. The two police who got killed only made it worse."

"Yeah, but if they don't know who y'all are, I don't see why you would still have to leave."

"Because it's better to be safe than sorry. You already know how them crackas is. You see what happened to that nigga who killed the tow police up there in Tampa. They locked up everybody who they thought was associated with him. Shit, they charged the girl who was with him with some shit that a ma'fucker ain't been charged with in forty years."

"Damn!"

"Yeah, it's alright for them to shoot you, but let one of them get killed, them ma'fuckers lose their minds."

"Alright, well listen. Promise me that when you do leave, you'll let me know you're going."

"I can do that."

"So promise me."

"Alright, I promise."

"Good, now let me give you something else to think about," she said before massaging him back to hardness, and after looking up at him seductively, she lowered her head and took him in her mouth.

***

"Alright, let's do it again," Curt said as he headed for the door.

"Do it again!" Tamaya screamed. "Curt, we've done it at least ten times already and all you keep doing is repeating the same thing over and over."

"And I'm gon keep repeating it til we got it right," Curt replied. "What you think this is a game?"

"No, but it's four o'clock in the damn morning. It ain't like we gon rob the bank tomorrow."

"No, but this is only one part of it. We still have to scope it out. After that, we have to make sure we got at least two escape routes, and that ain't even including stealing a car."

"Damn, you talkin like it's a job."

"That's exactly what it is, and if your ass want to stay out of jail, you'd better start acting like it."

"Alright, but can we at least take a break? I mean, it's four o'clock in the morning and we up in here on some G.I. Joe type shit."

"Yeah, but you gon be thanking me when we're sitting up in this ma'fucker counting our money."

"You know, looking at you, nobody would ever believe that you was on this type of shit. Shit, if I didn't see it for myself, I wouldn't have believed it."

"So what type of shit you thought I was on?"

"I don't know, but you definitely don't look like a nigga who be robbing banks."

"Yeah, well, I never would've thought you was down

for something like this."

"Oh, I'm bout a lot things you wouldn't believe."

"Like what?"

"Well, I drove out of town with a car full of dope before."

"You and who?"

"Me by myself."

"And what you call out of town?"

"Dayton, Ohio."

"Damn, you a rida, huh?"

"Damn right, and if I fucks with you, I'm all in."

"Oh, so you fucks with me?"

"What you think?"

"Shit, I didn't know. For all I know, you're just doing it for the money."

"That's part of the reason, but I also don't want to see you go to jail. I mean, true enough I misjudged you, but from what I've learned about you so far, I'm mad at myself for not getting to know you sooner."

"Damn, you feelin me like that?"

"You think I'd be in here with you practicing how to rob a bank, if I wasn't?"

"Well, you got a point," Curt said smiling and suddenly stepping closer to her, he pulled her close before kissing her.

"Hey, I thought we're supposed to be practicing?" She said jokingly.

"We are, that was just the intermission."

"Well, if you keep doing that, we gon be doing some practicing but it ain't gon be for robbing no bank."

"Shit, I ain't got no problem with that."

"I bet you don't, but right now we got work to do."

CHAPTER 30

"Hey, Ray Ray!"

"Yeah, man, what's up?"

"You feel like going to get something to eat?" Trigga asked after walking out of the room.

"Nigga, its four o'clock in the damn morning, where you gon get something to eat?"

"From the Royal Castle right up the street on 125th Street and 7th Avenue."

"Damn, we just passed by there. Why you ain't stop then?"

"Come on, nigga, don't act like you don't know what time it is. I mean, it ain't like I wouldn't do it for you."

"Alright man, what you want?"

"Two steak and eggs breakfast with hash browns, and you can get whatever you want."

"Oh, I know damn well I'm gon get what I want," Ray Ray replied while grabbing the car keys off the table, and walking towards Trigga, he held out his hands.

"What?"

"The money, nigga, cause I know damn well you don't think I'm buying breakfast. Shit, I ain't fuckin the bitch."

"Damn, it's like that?"

"Look, you gon give me the money or what?"

"Man, here, and you know that's fucked up," Trigga said while pulling some money from his pocket and after handing him a fifty dollar bill Ray Ray turned and headed for the door.

"Oh, and make sure the eggs are scrambled!" Trigga screamed. Without looking back, Ray Ray opened the door and stepped out into the crisp morning air.

Man, I don't believe this shit, he said to himself while walking to the car and finally approaching it with the keys in hand, he opened the door before climbing behind the wheel. Fumbling with the keys, he finally managed to get the key in the ignition and after starting it up, he adjusted the radio before putting the car in gear and driving off.

Easing out into 7th Avenue, he headed north while thinking about the big booty dancer from earlier, and as the reality hit him that he was out at four in the morning going for something to eat, he wished that he'd brought her home with him. Stopping at the light on 111th Street and 7th Avenue, he noticed a car pulling up behind him with its high beams on and he quickly adjusted the rearview mirror to keep the light from blinding him. He waited for the light to change. Suddenly, out of the corner of his eye, he noticed movements through the passenger window, and the moment he spotted the man wearing a ski mask and carrying an assault weapon, the man fired.

Instinctively, Ray Ray stepped on the gas, but not before being hit in the right arm, which rendered it useless. Round after round tore through the car and into him and unable to maintain control of the car, he veered sharply across the intersection and headed straight for the Church's Chicken restaurant on the corner. The sounds of the twisted metal and broken glass echoed loudly as the car crashed through the front of the restaurant before coming to a stop against the front counter.

Ray Ray could hear the sirens in the distance, but any hope of help reaching him in time was quickly dashed as the assailants ran to the driver's side, raised his gun, and fired point blank into the side of his face.

***

"Go! Go! Go!" Blue screamed as soon as he climbed in the car, and after quickly driving off, Craig looked around nervously for any signs of the police.

"So, what's up? We going back to the diamonds?"

"Hell, nah! The police gon be all round this bitch in a minute and the last thing a nigga gon want to do it get caught out here on the streets. Turn here!" He suddenly screamed as Craig drove cautiously down the backstreets, and suddenly realizing that they still had the murder weapon in the car, they became extra careful.

"So, where we headed?" Craig asked.

"Back to the apartments."

"What about Trigga?"

"We gon have to deal with him later."

"Wait a minute! Man, that nigga gon snap when he finds out about Ray Ray."

"He'll be alright. Besides, how he gon know we had something to do with it? The fucked up thing about robbing is that the robber don't remember everybody he robbed, but I bet you that everybody he's robbed remembers him."

"Oh, I see what you're saying. They done robbed so many people that they ain't gon be able to figure out who did it?'

"Yeah, and he gon fuck 'round and we gon be running down on his ass."

"I know that's right," Craig said while making a right turn onto 103rd and finally approaching the Silver Blue Lakes Apartments, he slowed down before turning up into the parking lot.

"You think I should park round back?"

"Yeah, cause a ma'fucker would have to drive through the parking lot to see it."

"Alright," Craig said as he drove around the side of the building. Quickly spotting a parking spot up ahead, he pulled in and parked.

"Damn, how the fuck we gon get the gun upstairs without somebody seeing us?" Blue suddenly asked.

"Shit, ain't nobody ain't out here this time of morning."

"Just cause you don't see nobody, don't mean that don't nobody see you," Blue shot back. "You already know that ma'fuckers don't miss nothing round here, and trust me, all closed eyes ain't sleep."

"Yeah, I feel you, so you want to leave it in the car till later?"

"We really ain't got no choice," Blue said and after making the decision, he laid the AK across the backseat before covering it with some clothes he found on the floor. "I'll come back once most of these ma'fuckers go to work."

"Alright, that'll work. You ready?"

"Yeah, let's go," Blue said before opening the door and stepping out of the car, and with Craig right behind him, they headed for the apartment. Finally reaching the door, Craig opened it before walking inside. Exhausted from the night's activities, Blue plopped down on the couch as Craig headed to the room for some much needed rest.

***

"What's going on?" Detective Nelson asked after noticing an uptick in activity inside the station.

"There's been a shooting."

"Where?"

"Northwest Miami-Dade."

"Do you have a location?"

"Yeah, just give me a minute. Ah, here it is, it's on 111th street and 7th Avenue."

"Any fatalities?"

"Only one confirmed so far. The call came in three minutes ago and it's reported that multiple shots were fired."

"Any suspects?"

"None reported, but patrols are conducting a blanket search of the area. All vehicles are being stopped and background checks are being done on the drivers."

"Alright, well I guess there's not much more they can do

for now. What's the status on the tag we sent to the feds for identification?"

"No word yet and even though the technician assured me that he'd do all he could do, he was doubtful of any positive results."

"What about the facial recognition search on the two women from the bank?"

"No hits, which means that neither of them has a record."

"Damn! We've got two dead policemen with no leads, and no suspects." Detective Nelson said in frustration.

"Hey, Detective!" Officer Chambers yelled out before walking up.

"Yeah, what's up?"

"Well, I was thinking about those two women from the bank and I think I've figured out a way to find out who they are."

"Alright, let's hear it."

"Well, for one, for them to be in the bank, they either have accounts there or they're accomplices."

"And how will you determine which?" Detective Nelson asked.

"By cross-referencing the time of their transaction with the time from the surveillance tapes."

"Huh?"

"What I did was, I went back and viewed the surveillance tapes a week prior to the robbery and those same two women can be seen inside the bank."

"So, they probably have accounts there?"

"It's a good possibility, but right now, I'm narrowing the scope by matching the time of their transaction with the time from the surveillance tape."

"Can you do that?"

"Yeah, I just need to look at what time they reached the counter from the surveillance tapes. Then, I cross reference it with the transactions done around the same time. I'll narrow the suspect pool considerably, and who knows, we may just get lucky."

"Well, you continue to explore those options because it may be the best shot we got. If you need any help, just let me know."

"Okay," Officer Chambers replied before turning to walk off.

"Oh, and Chambers," Detective Nelson said stopping him in his tracks, "Nice work."

"Thank you, sir."

After watching him go, Detective Nelson hurried into his office and closed the door behind him.

CHAPTER 31

"Damn, where this nigga at!" Trigga screamed while climbing out of bed. "It don't take that long to go right up the street."

"He needs to hurry up cause I'm hungry," the green eyed beauty replied.

"Yeah, but don't worry cause I'm gon get you something to eat," Trigga shot back before stepping into his pants, and as soon as he sat down and grabbed his shoes, he heard someone banging on the front door.

"Man, who the fuck is that banging on my damn door?"

"It might be your friend with the food."

"Nah, cause he's got a key."

"Well, I don't know," she said as the banging continued, and growing angrier by the minute, Trigga rushed out of the room to go find out.

"Alright, I'm coming, damn!" He screamed while approaching the door, and suddenly snatching it open, he came face to face with his next door neighbor.

"Man, what the fucks wrong with you banging on my door this time of morning?"

"Listen, my girl just came home from work and she said she saw your car inside the Church's Chicken Restaurant up the street." He replied.

"She what?" Trigga asked trying to make sense of what he'd just heard.

"She said that your car crashed through the front of the Church's Chicken Restaurant up the street."

"Is she sure it was my car?"

"Yeah, why you think I came over here? I mean, I told her that I didn't know if you were driving."

"Nah, Ray Ray got my—oh shit!" He screamed as the implications suddenly hit him. Running across the parking lot, he looked up the street and saw the police lights in the distance. *Damn!* He thought to himself before running back to his apartment. With a million thoughts running through his mind, he turned to his neighbor.

"Hey, man, I need a ride up the street to find out what's going on."

"Alright, just let me go tell my girl that I'll be right back," the neighbor replied.

"Yeah, alright, and by the time you get back, I'll be ready to go," Trigga said before rushing into the apartment.

"So, who was that?" The stripper asked as soon as he walked through the door.

"Just hurry up and get dressed."

"What's wrong?"

"I think something's happened to my friend."

"Something like what?"

"Shit, if I knew that, I wouldn't have to go find out now, so hurry up."

"Alright, but damn, don't get mad at me. I ain't did nothing."

"Yeah, I know, I just got a lot on my mind right now." Trigga said while trying to figure out what could've possibly happened. Seconds later, they were headed for his neighbor's car, and no closer to figuring out what could've happened. he knew that he'd find out soon enough as they climbed into the car started it up and drove out of the parking lot.

***

"What time is it?" Snag asked while lying in bed watching Crystal get dressed for work.

"Five o'clock."

"And what time you get off?"

"Just asking."

"Oh, so you ain't gon miss me?" She asked playfully.

"Hell, yeah! What about you, you gon miss me?"

"Maybe."

"Maybe?" He said before suddenly hugging her from behind. Feeling his semi-hard dick rubbing up against her ass, she pushed back into him while looking back at him seductively.

"Alright now, you better stop or I might not make it to work."

"Stop what?"

"Don't act crazy, you know."

"Nah, for real, what you talkin bout?"

"This," she said while reaching behind her back to grab his dick.

"Oh, that."

"Yeah, that," she replied playfully while turning to face him, and knowing that if she got hot now, there was no way she'd made it to work on time, she walked away.

"What's wrong?"

"Nothing."

"So, why you walked away?"

"Cause if I don't, I'll end up being late for work, if I make it at all." She said smiling.

"Well, that won't be a bad thing."

"No, it won't, but I need my job."

"What if I'd paid you to stay home?"

"Then what I'm gon do when I lose my job and the money runs out?"

"I'll give you some more."

"It sounds good, but I think I'll stick with the fo'sho money."

"So what, I'm gon see you when get off?"

"You better or I'm gon be pissed. What you getting into today anyway?"

"I don't know, probably just sit round tryin to figure out what I'm gon do next."

"Well, don't forget what you promised me."

"I won't. You just don't have me waiting all day for you to get home."

"Believe me, nobody's gonna be happier to get home than me."

"Is that right?"

"Yeah, that's right," she said before reaching out to fondle him through his pants, and you better be here when I get here."

"Alright, well you got my cell number so call me," she said before grabbing her purse. Heading for the door, and after walking out, Snag waited for Curt to come downstairs. Deciding to take a quick shower, he headed for the bathroom and suddenly weighing their options in his head, he knew that he had to talk with Curt because if not, they'd never get a chance to enjoy the money they'd worked so hard to get.

***

"Alright, look, I'm tired," Tamaya said while taking a seat on the edge of the bed. "It's five in the morning and we've been doing this since two. Don't you think three hours is enough?"

"Yeah, for now," Curt replied. "I mean, you did do better than I expected."

"Wait a minute! What you mean I did better than you expected?"

"Just what I said, for somebody who ain't never robbed a bank you, did good. The real test gon come when we go up in the bank."

"Yeah, well, I'm gon handle mine."

"Alright, but remember, we still gotta pick which bank we gon hit and then we gotta do surveillance."

"Do what?"

"Surveillance. That's when you scope out the area around

the bank just in case something goes wrong."

"Oh, sort of like what happened last time?"

"Yeah, something like that. Only we didn't anticipate two police getting killed."

"I'm sure y'all didn't, but when you plan on doing all that?"

"Well, we can pick a bank while sittin here, and as far as the surveillance, we can do that anytime. Oh, and we still gotta get a car but I can steal one the night before."

"Alright, so when you plan on doing it?"

"What, robbing the bank?"

"Yeah."

"Well, I want to do it within a week."

"Damn, you ain't bullshittin, huh?"

"Nah, cause I figure that the last thing the police gon expect is for us to hit another bank so soon. Especially after what happened during the last one."

"Alright, but suppose they're expecting it?"

"That's what this is for," he replied while picking up the AK and cradling it in his arms.

"Look, we ain't tryin to get in no shootouts with the police."

"No, but if shit gets crazy, I'm all in. I mean, it's either that or end up on death row."

"Ain't nobody going to no death row so stop talkin crazy. We gon go in, do what we gotta do, and leave with the money. It's that simple."

"I hope it is," Curt replied smiling. "I mean, if shit went like that every time, I'd rob a bank every week."

"We ain't trying to rob a bank every week. We just trying

to hit this one and get as much money as we can!"

"Yeah, I'm feelin that, but at the same time, I'm hungrier than a ma'fucker."

"Me too."

"So what, you gon cook something?"

"For what when I got something for you to eat right here." She said before pulling up her skirt.

"Oh, you got jokes, huh?"

CHAPTER 32

Standing with the stripper at the edge of the yellow crime scene tape, Trigga watched as the police pulled his bullet riddled car out of the restaurant. Covered by a tarp, he could only imagine what Ray Ray's body looked like. He knew all too well how the game was played, and if you got caught slipping, it often cost you your life.

Someone had caught Ray Ray by surprise as he sat at the light and either dead or dying, he'd crashed the car through the front of the restaurant. He knew that the police would eventually want to talk to him once they ran the tag. But he wasn't worried because his alibi was standing next to him. His friend had just left his apartment to go get something to eat. Who knows what happened after that. One thing was for certain though; he was going to find out who was responsible if it was the last thing he did.

Looking around at the faces in the crowd, it took everything in him to conceal his anger, and while suddenly thinking about who might've been responsible, several names came to mind. The life of a robber was a hectic one, but somebody had to do it and reflecting on the few names that popped into his head, one of them stood out more than the rest. Ray Ray had tried to warn him about Blue, but he hadn't listened and now look what happened. Right then, he made a vow to never make that mistake again because he knew that if he did, it could all be over in a blink of an eye. Grabbing the stripper's hand, he suddenly turned and walked off while pulling her behind him. After walking back to the neighbor's, car they climbed in.

"So, what's up? That's your car?" The neighbor asked before starting it.

"Yeah, that's it."

"Well, what happened?"

"I don't know, but the police gon be coming to my apartment soon."

"For what? I mean, you ain't had nothing to do with that. I'll even tell 'em that you were home when my girl came home and told me about it."

"Yeah, but the car's registered to me so they gon wanna know who was driving."

"Alright, but if you need me, let me know."

"Yeah, alright," Trigga replied as they drove down 7th Avenue, and after finally pulling up in the Diamonds parking lot, he hopped out and headed for his apartment with the stripper right on his heels.

"Look, can I just get my money so I can get out of here? I ain't got time for this," she said as soon as they walked into the apartment.

"Yeah, just give me a minute," Trigga replied before walking into his room. Seconds later, he returned carrying a hand full of cash.

"Here, that's twenty five hundred dollars."

"But you only owe me a thousand."

"Yeah, I know, the other grand is for you to come back tonight after you get off work."

"What about the other five hundred?"

"I'm giving it to you because I like you," he said while managing a smile.

"Yeah, well, I like you too and thanks."

"Mmm hmm! Just don't make me come looking for your ass."

"You won't have to. I promise. Matter of fact, I get off work round three o'clock so I should be here no later than three thirty."

"Alright, well I gotta few things I need to take care of today so I'll holla at you later."

"Alright," she replied before heading for the door, and after watching her walk out, Trigga rushed over to the hall closet, grabbed his AK and after taking a seat on the couch, he inserted the clip and chambered a round. After making a quick phone call, he hung up after a brief conversation and thought about his friends. Suddenly feeling somewhat responsible for what happened, he vowed to make whoever was involved pay dearly.

***

"Any progress on that thing you were working on?" Detective Nelson asked after walking over to where Officer Chambers sat behind his computer.

"I've narrowed the list down to fifteen names so far," Officer Chambers replied.

"Why so many? I mean, I thought you said that you'd look at the time from the surveillance tape and then cross-reference it with the transactions made around the same time."

"That's exactly what I did, but the computer doesn't distinguish one transaction from the next one. All it does is record them chronologically in the order they were completed."

"Alright, so how are we gonna find out who these women are?"

"Well, I thought about faxing the names over to the Department of Motor Vehicles for a list of addresses."

"Good thinking, but the D.M.V. doesn't open til eight. It's now ten minutes to six, so that gives us a little over two hours before we can have the information."

"Unless..."

"Unless what?"

"Unless I can call the supervisor of the D.M.V. and explain the situation to them. Who knows, maybe we can get the information faster."

"Alright, and I'll see if I can narrow the list even more."

"Good, now what's the word on the shooting?" Detective Nelson suddenly asked changing the subject.

"Well, from what I got somebody was sitting at the light on 111th street and 7th Avenue in Northwest Miami-Dade when someone opened fired on him with an automatic weapon causing him to lose control of his car and crash though the front of a restaurant."

“Let me guess, the victim’s black?”

“Yeah, but how’d you know?”

“Because it’s become almost routine, and I’m willing to bet that the shooter was black also.”

“As far as I know, there are no known suspects.”

“Yeah, but when he’s caught, I’m almost certain he’ll be black,” Detective Nelson repeated.

“Maybe, but that’s homicide’s job to figure out. Mine is to find out who killed the two officers and robbed those banks,” Officer Chambers replied.

“Well, I see you learn fast.”

“That’s because I’ve got good teacher.”

“Yeah, well anyway, let me go make this phone call to see if I can make something happen.”

“Okay, and I’ll continue to narrow this list down some more. In fact, I’ll just print out the names so that if you get the go ahead from the D.M.V. supervisor, we can fax ‘em over immediately.”

“Sounds like a plan to me. Now, let’s put it in effect,” Detective Nelson said before turning and walking off. After seeing him go, Officer Chambers immersed himself in his work.

***

“Curt, we gotta hurry up or I’m gon be later for work,” Tamaya said looking back at him.

“Alright,” he replied while continuing to pound his dick in and out of her, and suddenly grabbing her waist and pulling her into him, he came flooding her insides. “Damn!”

he screamed before collapsing on top of her. Trying to catch his breath, he rolled over onto his back.

"Boy, you gon have me late for work," she said while climbing out of bed.

"At least it's for a good reason."

"Oh, so what I'm gon tell my supervisor? That I'm late cause I was getting some dick."

"Yeah, I mean why not?"

"Boy, you crazy for real. Them people don't care about that?"

"Well, they should."

"Mmm hmm! Anyway, what you doing today?"

"I don't know yet, why?"

"Cause I remember you said something about us having to figure out which bank we gon hit."

"Yeah, but I can do that while you're at work. You gon have to go with me to scope out the area just in case something happens."

"Alright, so when you want to do that?"

"We can do it when you get off work."

"Alright, and when do you plan to steal the car?"

"Well, I can do that the night before we hit the bank, but we still need to practice."

"For what? I got—"

"Tamaya, listen," he said cutting her off. "The last thing we need is for us to be inside bank and you start making mistakes. Not only can it cause us to go to jail, but it could also get us killed."

"Alright, but I'm tellin you, I ain't getting up at no two o'clock in the morning no more."

"Oh, no?" Curt asked with a smirk.

"Boy, you know what I'm talkin bout. Now I gotta go to work all tired."

"Shit, you ain't gotta go."

"I wish I didn't."

"Well, you can rest when you get home."

"Mmm hmm! Like you gon let me. Anyway, let me go take a shower so I can get ready to get out of here."

"Want me to wash your back?"

"Boy, no! Cause if you get in the shower with me, I'll never make it to work."

"Yeah, alright, go ahead and I'll take one after you."

"Okay," Tamaya replied before walking into the bathroom. After deciding against showering with her, Curt started to wonder about Snag and the situation they'd gotten themselves into. Minutes later, Tamaya walked out of the bathroom, and after drying off, she began getting dressed.

"And don't be in there all day," she said jokingly as he headed for the bathroom.

"Yeah, alright," he replied before jumping in the shower himself. Ten minutes later, they were both dressed and ready to go.

"I should be home around four o'clock."

"Alright, and I'll come up when I see your car."

"Okay," she replied before walking out the door and down the stairs. After walking to her car, climbing in, and driving off, Curt headed for his apartment.

CHAPTER 33

"Damn, nigga, bout time! I thought I was gon have to come looking for you," Snag said as soon as he walked through the door.

"Yeah, whatever, you just saying that cause Crystal's gon to work."

"Nah, I'm saying it cause the police are looking for us and we need to sit down and figure out what the fuck we gon do."

"Ain't nothing to figure out."

"If we stay here, them crackas gon find us eventually."

"Okay, and if we go somewhere, where we gon go?"

"Well, I got people in Georgia, so if anything, that's where I'm going," Curt said.

"So what about the girls?"

"What you mean, what about 'em?"

"We gon take 'em with us or what? That's what I mean, cause if them crackas ever find somebody who saw their car, you already know they gon come holla at 'em."

"True, but at the same time, it's gon look kind of suspicious if they just quit their jobs and leave town all of a sudden."

"Man, look, we need to be worryin bout us. We're the ones who killed the damn police and robbed the banks.

"Yeah, but we also got them involved."

"How you figure? 'Cause I don't remember telling them to come pick us up."

"No, but you ain't tell 'em to drive off and leave us either."

"Alright, but man, let me ask you a question. How long do you think two hundred grand gon last us? I mean, really..."

"Shit, I don't know but why you ask me that?"

"Cause you're sitting here trying to figure out what we gon do and where we gon go, and I'm trying to figure out what we gon do bout money once what we got runs out."

"Look, we can't worry bout that right now cause I mean, if push comes to shove, we can always hit another bank. Right now, we need to be tryin to get as far away from Miami as possible."

"And how we supposed to do that? Cause my car definitely won't make it out the state."

"Well, we can get a car from anywhere. Shit, we can steal one if we have to."

"Alright, but it still comes back to what we gon do and where we gon go," Snag said and as they stood in Curt's living room debating their future, Curt gave no indication that he was planning to rob another bank.

***

"Hey, Blue!"

"Yeah, what's up?" He asked after being startled out of his sleep.

"Man, tighten up, we need to go holla at that nigga Chris out there in Opa-Locka bout our shit."

"Alright, just let me wash up right quick," he said before heading for the bathroom.

While waiting for his friend, Craig walked back into this bedroom to grab his Glock .40 pistol, and after inserting the clip and chambering a round, he tucked it in his pants, "Damn, nigga, hurry up!" he screamed while walking out into the living room. Seconds later, Blue joined him.

"What's up, you ready?"

"Yeah, I'm just waiting on you."

"Well, let's go," Blue said before heading for the door and after following him outside, Craig walked to the car, climbed in, and started it up.

"Damn! We forgot to take this shit out the car," Blue said while reaching into the backseat and removing the clothes from on top of the AK.

"Yeah, I forgot all about it," Craig replied.

"So what's up, you want to take it upstairs?"

"Nah, fuck it cause if that nigga Chris start talking crazy, I'm gon let him have it."

"Well, you know I'm bout that," Blue replied as Craig put the car in gear and drove out the parking lot. Making a quick right on 17th Avenue, he drove north before coming to a stop at the light on 119th Street minutes later. Turning left, he drove to 22nd Avenue and after making another right, he continued North while making sure to obey all traffic laws.

Suddenly making a right on 136th Street, he passed the Burger King Restaurant before pulling over in front of the third house on the left. Cutting the car off, he got out and headed for the door as Blue chambered a round in the AK and scanned the street carefully. Knocking several times, Craig waited patiently for someone to answer the door and seconds later, someone did as the door opened slightly.

"Yeah, what's up?" A voice asked.

"Yeah, I'm looking for Chris."

"Who you?"

"Craig."

"Craig?"

"Yeah, from out the Silver Blue Lakes Apartments."

"Oh, Craig! Damn, nigga, what's up?" Chris asked while pulling the door all the way open.

"Hey, man I need to holla at you about something."

"Alright, well come in," Chris said while stepping to the side, and after walking into the house, Craig waited as he closed the door behind him.

"Man, this shit gotta be important, you know what time it is?"

"Yeah, I know.

"Alright, what's up?"

"Last night, somebody gave you something that belongs to me," Craig said getting straight to the point.

"What?"

"I got robbed for eighty stacks plus a brick and a half, and last night while sitting in the parking lot of the King of Diamonds, I saw this nigga name Trigga give it to you."

"Wait a minute! And how do you know that that's what

he gave me?"

"Cause it's still in the black bag I had it in. Now, I don't know what kind of arrangements y'all made, but I came to holla at you to get my shit back."

"Well, look, I don't know what's going on between y'all two but man, I ain't got nothing to do with it. I'm just out here trying to get some money."

"I feel you and we go way back that's why I figured I could come talk to you."

"Yeah, man, but damn, I told him to come by to pick up his money this morning," Chris said in frustration. "I mean, what I'm gon tell him?'

"Honestly, I don't care what you tell him. I just want my shit back."

"And what if I say *no*?"

"Then I'll respect it, but you know it ain't gon be over," Craig replied.

"Yeah, and we go too far back for that bullshit."

"Mmm hmm! So, what's up?" Craig asked matter of factly.

"Damn, dogg! You know what, fuck it! I'll let him know that I ain't down with the bullshit he on, and if he don't like it, oh well. Wait right here," he said as he turned and headed for the kitchen and seconds later, he returned carrying a black bag. "Here, and you need to be careful from now on."

"Yeah, man, and I appreciate it," Craig replied before unzipping the bag.

"Oh, it's all there," Chris said as Craig checked the contents. Satisfied that everything was as it was supposed to be, he zipped that bag closed before throwing it over his shoulder.

"So, you good?"

"Yeah, but if I gave you my number and asked you to call me when he comes by, would you?"

"Man, I ain't trying to get caught up in that."

"Alright, I respect that. Anyway, I'm gon go ahead and get out of here but I'll holla," Craig said before opening the door. After walking outside, he headed for his car.

Meanwhile, after closing the door behind him, Chris began mentally preparing himself to deal with Trigga.

***

"Oh, and you think the nigga Blue had something to do with it?" Chevy asked as they traveled down 27th Avenue. "Shit, all the niggas y'all done robbed it could've been anybody."

"Maybe, but I still think it was that nigga Blue and I'm gon show him that he ain't the only one living like that."

"Alright, so where we headed at now?"

"To holla at a nigga name Chris out of Opa Locka."

"What's up with him, he straight?"

"Yeah, I just gotta holla at him bout some money. After that, I want to ride through Silver Blue Lakes to see if them niggas out."

"Alright," Chevy replied as they approached 135th Street.

"You gon make a right by the Burger King," Trigga said, and after changing lanes, Chevy drove through the intersection before making a quick right.

"It's the third house on the left."

"I got you," Chevy said while pulling over to the side of the road.

"This shouldn't take long," Trigga shot back before getting out of the car and heading for the door. Then, after knocking several times, he waited for someone to answer. Receiving no response, he decided to knock again and as soon as he raised his hand, the door opened.

"What's up?" Chris asked.

"I came to get my money," Trigga replied.

"Alright, come in," and after stepping aside Trigga walked in.

"Why you ain't tell me that you robbed a nigga for that shit?" Chris suddenly said while closing the door.

"What I do is my business. Besides, what's that gotta do with anything?"

"Everything, cause I know the nigga you robbed."

"So!"

"So, the nigga just left here and you know what else?"

"Nah, what?"

"I gave him his shit back."

"Wait a minute! What you mean you gave him the shit back?"

"Look, the nigga you robbed followed you to the King of Diamonds, and he was in the parking lot watching us when you gave me the shit."

"Alright, but what's that gotta do with the money you owe me?"

"You ain't heard nothing I said? I gave him the shit back so I don't owe you nothing."

"Man, you got me fucked up!" Trigga screamed. "What

you and him got going on is on y'all, but I want my money."

"Man, listen."

"Nah, nigga you listen," Trigga said while suddenly pulling his gun. "Now, you gon give me my money or shit's about to get ugly up in here."

"Nigga, you gon come up in my shit and pull a gun on me?"

"Fuck that! I want my ma'fuckin money."

"Well, you know what? Fuck you, I ain't giving you shit."

"Oh, no, well guess what? Fuck you!" Trigga screamed and without another word, he raised his gun and fired. The bullet tore into Chris face before blowing out the back of his head. As this body slumped to the floor, Trigga fired two more rounds into his chest.

Tell me I can't get my money, you got me fucked up, he said to himself while stepping over the body. Suddenly rushing down the hall, he began searching for Chris' stash. Quickly finding it in his bedroom closet, Trigga snatched a pillowcase off the bed and began filling it with cash. After placing the last of the money in the pillowcase, he frantically searched the other three rooms and finding nothing, he grabbed the pillowcase full of cash and headed for the door.

Hurrying outside, he walked to the car and got in. Then, as Chevy pulled off, he thought about what Chris had said, which only confirmed his suspicions about Blue.

CHAPTER 34

"Damn, nigga, what happened?" Chevy asked while driving away from the house.

"Nothing, just drive." Trigga replied.

"Well, if nothing happened, who was shooting?"

"Look, I'll explain everything once we get back to the apartment."

"Oh, so we ain't goin by the Silver Blue Lakes Apartments?"

"Nah, not right now. Just take me back to the apartments and I got you."

"Alright," Chevy replied while eyeing the pillowcase Trigga held between his legs, and while driving cautiously, he tried not to think about what may have happened back at the house.

Fifteen minutes later, they pulled into the parking lot of the Diamonds Apartments.

"Park in the front of my door," Trigga suddenly said as Chevy searched for somewhere to park and after pulling up in the front of the apartments, they both got out and headed inside.

"So, what's up, you gon tell me what happened?" Chevy asked as soon as the door closed behind them.

"Yeah, I murked that nigga," Trigga replied.

"You did what?"

"I said I murked that nigga."

"For what?"

"Cause he tried me that why. I go round there and the nigga gon tell me that I couldn't get paid."

"He ain't say why?"

"Yeah, something about he knows the nigga I robbed and that when the nigga stepped to him, he gave the shit to him."

"Hold up! You robbed a nigga and sold the shit to him? Then the nigga you robbed stepped to him so he gave him the shit back, and he had the nerve to tell you that you couldn't get paid?"

"Yeah, ain't that some shit?"

"Hell, yeah! So what you told him?"

"I ain't tell him shit, I slumped his ass and took this," Trigga said while holding up the pillowcase.

"So, you robbed him?"

"Damn right! How he gon get my shit and then tell me I can't get paid?"

"I feel you, but damn."

"Damn what? I mean, I told you I got you."

"Yeah, but it ain't bout that. Suppose somebody saw my car back at the house?"

"Nigga, with what I'm gon give you can buy another car," Trigga replied. "Now help me count this shit cause I still want to go through Silver Blue Lakes Apartments."

"Yeah, alright," Chevy said while watching Trigga pour out the contents of the bag in the middle of the living room, and as he squatted down and began separating the stacks of money, he knew that if he accepted the money from Trigga, he was accepting all the baggage that came with it.

***

"Alright, here's the deal," Detective Nelson said after bursting into the office. "I just got off the phone with the supervisor at the Department of Motor Vehicles and she's being a complete ass. I told her what we're trying to do and I even explained to her the situation down to the two police officers getting killed and she had the nerve to talk to me about confidentiality."

"So, will she do it?"

"No, she won't give it to us without a court order."

"Is she serious?"

"I'm afraid so. I mean, not even two dead officers could persuade her."

"Okay, how hard is it to get a court order?"

"For something like that, I don't know. Judge Blake is on vacation, and if I go before another judge, I'll have to convince him that the ends of justice are more important than protecting people's constitutional rights."

"Okay, well look. I've narrowed the list down to seven names and I might be able to get the addresses."

"How?"

"By making a few phone calls."

"To whom?"

"I know some people in the traffic division and just maybe I can get them to look up the names in their databases."

"It's worth a try," Detective Nelson said. "Meanwhile, I'll start contacting a few judges' secretaries to see if I can get in to see one of them. Then, I'll explain the situation to them and hopefully I can convince them how important this is."

"Alright, and here's a list of the names," Officer Chambers said while handing him a sheet of paper with the names listed on it. "While you're working on your end, I'll continue to work mine, and together we should be able to come up with something."

"I agree, now is anything else happening?"

"Other than a body being found in a house in Opa-Locka, no."

"Did you say a body was found in a house in Opa-Locka?"

"Yeah, someone named Hawthorne or something like that."

"Wait a minute! Christopher Hawthorne?"

"Yeah, you know him?"

"Yeah, a few years back I sent him to prison for robbing drug dealers. Rumor had it that when he got out, he started selling drugs himself."

"Well, karma's a bitch because they're looking at robbery as a possible motive."

"Son of a bitch."

"What?"

"Nothing, you know who got the call?"

"Yeah, Detective Shaw."

"Okay, thanks and give me a call the minute you find out anything." Detective Nelson said before rushing out of the office. As the door closed behind him, Officer Chambers picked up the phone and called his friend.

***

"Man, let me hit that," Curt said as he sat in his living room watching TV with Snag.

"Here, and turn the channel while you're at it," Snag replied while passing him the blunt.

"What you want to watch?"

"Shit, I don't know, just find something."

"Alright," Curt said before grabbing the remote and while channel surfing, he took a pull on the joint. After filling his lungs with the putrid smoke, he held his breath while continuing to browse through the channels. Suddenly spotting a breaking news story, he paused.

"What's that?"

"I don't know."

"Well, damn nigga turn it up," Snag said and as Curt turned up the volume, they listened to the reporter speaking.

> "Where the police are investigating a shooting that left one dead. Anyone with information is being urged to call the police. In another developing story the police are still searching for the two gunmen who killed two police offers while robbing the Barnett Bank located on 79th Street and

> Northeast 9th Avenue. They are also searching for an African American woman driving a red of maroon Toyota Camry with a Temporary Tag in the back window. While she is not being considered a suspect, the police would like to talk to her. If you know someone with a car fitting this description, please call the number on your screen and ask for Detective Nelson. You can be eligible for a reward. I'm Michael Criswell live in Northwest Miami-Dade, back to you."

"Oh, shit! Man, you heard what that ma'fucker said?" Snag asked excitedly.

"Hell, yeah! What you think I'm deaf?"

"Damn! Somebody must've seen her car when she picked us up."

"I don't know. I mean, I think they would've said something."

"Man, you should know by now that them ma'fuckas ain't gon tell you everything. They'll say that they just want to talk to her, but when they get her ass down to the station, it'll be something different."

"Alright, but she can't really tell 'em nothing."

"Nigga, is you crazy? You forgot that they was in the bank when we ran up in there."

"Nah, I ain't forgot," Curt replied. "But you also gotta remember that they went out of their way to pick us up so if they say anything bout us, they gon be telling on themselves."

"Fuck! This is all we need," Snag screamed in frustration.

"Look, panicking ain't go do us no good. What we need to do is figure out what we gon do about Tamaya and Crystal cause they gon trip when they find out."

"So what, you gon wait till they get home to tell 'em?"

"Hell, nah, I'm gon call Tamaya at work cause what if she's driving home and the police pull her over?"

"Yeah, but now what she gon do about the car?"

"We can worry about that later. Right now, we gon call her and let her know what's up."

"Alright," Snag replied, and as Curt pulled out his phone, he dialed Tamaya's number. Snag wondered to himself what else could possibly go wrong.

CHAPTER 35

Sitting in front of her computer, Tamaya could barely keep her eyes open. Getting up at two in the morning didn't seem so bad at first but now it was definitely taking a toll on her. To keep her mind occupied, she thought about Curt and the plans they were making, and if everything went as planned, she'd have more money than she'd ever imagined. The thought alone got her excited. Then there was Curt and the way he was and before she could finish her thought, her phone rang startling her. Caught off guard momentarily, she quickly regained her composure. After answering her phone, she smiled the minute she heard Curt's voice.

"Bout time! I ain't think you was gon call. Yeah, I'm hear half asleep and it's all your fault. Yea right, you the one that wanted to act like we were on some Navy Seal type shit. Oh, nah, the last part was straight. It's the getting up at two o'clock I'm talkin bout. Nah, I ain't talked to her since I've been to work, why? Say what? Wait a minute! Say that again. Oh, shit! Boy, what you mean don't panic? I remember what

I said but this is different. Them ma'fuckas described my damn car. I wouldn't be surprised if one of these ma'fuckas called the police on my ass. I can't believe this shit. Crystal gone lose her mind when she finds out. Oh, I know that but now what I'm gon do? I'm round here asking you where you gon go and now they're looking for my ass. What I'm do bout my damn car? Oh, you ain't gotta worry bout me driving it nowhere, but at the same time, I can't just leave it here. Shit, for all I know, they might show up at my damn job. When? Alright, but then what? What about my clothes and my other stuff? Yeah, alright. But you better hurry up cause this shit just fucked up my whole day an I definitely don't want to be here. Mmm hmm! I hear you. Alright bye," she said before hanging up, and while sitting there thinking about what Curt had just told her, she had no idea what she would do.

Suddenly feeling the need to talk to someone, she grabbed the phone and dialed Crystal's number. After a few rings, her friend answered.

"Hello! Yeah, what's up? Girl, are you sitting down? Well, I just got off the phone with Curt and he said that on the news, them crackas described my damn car. Talking bout they want to talk to me. Not even five minutes ago. Shit, I don't know. Somebody must've seen my car when we picked them up. Nah, they don't know who I am. If they did, I wouldn't be on the phone talking to you. Listen, ain't nobody going to jail. I just gotta figure out what I'm gon do now. Well, Curt and Snag are on the way to come pick me up. Girl, I ain't driving that car nowhere. Didn't you just hear me say that they were looking for it? Anyway, Curt said he would was gon take it somewhere til I can figure out what I'm gon do next. Nah, he gon take me to get some clothes from the apartments. Nah, you're good. It's me they want to talk to. Alright, well listen. When I get wherever I'm going, I'll call you and let you know where I'm at. Until then, don't talk to nobody bout nothing, and keep doing what you doing. Alright, and trust me, everything's gonna be alright. Mmm hmm! Bye." Tamaya said before hanging up and suddenly feeling less confident about the situation than she had let on, she stood and headed for the ladies' room. Walking in, she found an empty stall. Then rushing inside, she closed the door behind her and after taking a seat, she began shaking uncontrollably.

***

"So how much that is?" Trigga asked while pointing to the stack of money in Chevy's hand.

"Ten grand,"

"What about these stacks right here?"

"Fifty grand a piece."

"Alright, and that's what, five stacks?"

"Yeah,"

"So altogether it's two hundred and sixty grand."

"Damn, nigga, you done came the fuck up!" Chevy screamed.

"True, but fifty of it's yours."

"Hold up, fifty what?" Chevy asked curiously.

"Fifty grand."

"What!"

"Well, I told you I got you didn't I?"

"Yeah, but damn I ain't know you was talkin bout giving me fifty grand."

"Well, before we went to that nigga house, I didn't know I was gon have two hundred and something grand." Trigga said as he set the ten grand to the side and began stuffing the rest of his money into the pillowcase.

"Man, I can't believe I got fifty grand." Chevy said to himself before reaching down to pick up his money and while watching Trigga stuff his money into the pillowcase, he realized he needed somewhere to put his.

"Hey, you got a bag or something to put this in?"

"Yeah, just give me a minute," Trigga replied before heading towards his room and seconds later, he returned carrying a plastic Winn Dixie bag. "Here, this is all I got."

"Shit, that'll work," Chevy said before taking the bag from him, and after putting his money inside, he wrapped it up while looking up at Trigga.

"Alright, now what?"

"What you mean, I told you I wanted ride through the Silver Blue Lake Apartments."

"Okay, so what we waitin on?"

"Cause I need to holla at you bout something first. You know I ain't goin over there to talk to them niggas, right? I mean, I already told you that I think the nigga Blue had something to do with Ray Ray getting killed so I'm blasting on sight."

"Look, if I wasn't down with you, I would've drove off when I heard the shooting at the house in Opa-Locka."

***

"Hey, grab your stuff and let's go." Detective Nelson said after rushing into the office.

"Why, what's up?" Officer Chambers replied.

"I just got the court order signed, and believe me, it wasn't easy. As soon as we leave the D.M.V., we'll start interviewing the people on the list and hopefully we'll get lucky."

"Alright, just let me call my people and let 'em know that we don't need the help, at least not right now," Officer Chambers said while grabbing the phone, and as he spoke briefly to someone on the other end, Detective Nelson was already contemplating his next move.

Minutes later, Officer Chambers hung up. Quickly shutting off his computer, he turned to face the detective.

"I'm ready when you are."

"Alright, come on," Detective Nelson said while stepping out into the hall and following him out, Officer Chambers listened carefully.

"The first thing I want you to do is go down to the armory and grab a vest and another weapon, preferably something with more rounds. I'll call ahead and let the supervisor know that I have the court order and I'm on my way back. Now, we don't know if any of these people are involved in the bank robberies or not but we'll be extremely cautious when approaching their residences. We have two cop killers on the loose and our job is to bring 'em in regardless of what it takes, do you understand?"

"Yes, sir."

"Good, now I'll meet you at the car in five minutes," Detective Nelson said before walking off, and after watching him leave, Officer Chambers rushed downstairs to the armory. Exactly five minutes later, Detective Nelson arrived at his county issued sedan to find Officer Chambers waiting for him.

"I see that punctuality is one of your strong points, huh?"

"Yeah, you can say that," Officer Chambers replied with a smirk.

"Alright, you ready?"

"Yeah."

"Well, let's do this," Detective Nelson said while climbing behind the wheel and after starting it up, and putting it in, gear they drove out the parking lot.

CHAPTER 36

"Man, is you crazy!" Snag screamed. "You just saw the news and you heard them say that the police are looking for her, and you talkin about driving the car somewhere."

"What else we gon do, huh? Tell me that cause we can't just leave the car at her job. It's bad enough that she ain't gon be able to go back to work for a minute."

""Don't you think that's gon look kind of strange?"

"What?"

"Her not showing up to work all of a sudden."

"She could tell 'em that she's taking a vacation or something."

"Just out the blue? Why she can't just act like nothing happened? I mean, when the police find her, she could just tell 'em that she don't know nothing."

"Man, listen, the last thing we want is for her to open her mouth in a room full of detectives. They'll chew her ass up and spit her out. Like it ain't nothing, you got niggas who been in the streets all their lives and they can't deal with them ma'fuckers so what makes you think she gon be able to?"

"Alright, so we go pick her up and you take the car somewhere. Then what we gon do?"

"Shit, I don't know but I know that we can't just sit round and do nothing. Now what we need to do is get a room for a few days while we figure out what we gon do."

""'Alright, but what about Crystal?"

"She's good I mean it's Tamaya's car somebody saw so that's why they want to talk to her.

"Yeah, but don't you think them crackas saw them together inside the bank?"

"What?"

"You must've forgot that they got cameras inside the bank."

"Damn! I forgot all about them. You know what, that might be how they saw Tamaya's car. Remember they said on the news that they were looking for a woman driving a red or maroon Toyota Camry with a temporary tag in the window."

"Yeah."

"So we assumed that somebody saw the car, but what if they saw the car leaving the bank's parking lot on the surveillance camera?"

"It's possible."

"Yeah, and if that's the case, she could tell em she was scared and just wanted to get out of there."

"That shit sounds good, but how we gone know if somebody saw her car or they saw it on the surveillance camera? That's the question."

"Yeah, it is," Snag replied as Curt pulled up in front of

the Lindsey Hopkins Building located on 20th Street and 7th Avenue, and just as he was about to get out of the car, Curt spotted Tamaya hurrying towards them.

"Boy, what took y'all so long?" She asked while climbing into the backseat.

"Damn, we left as soon as we got off the phone with you."

"Yeah, well it felt like a long time ago."

"Girl, you're just paranoid."

"Damn right I'm paranoid. Let me tell it everybody's watching me."

"Girl, ain't nobody watching you. Don't nobody even know what's going on. Anyway, where's your car?"

"Around the corner in the student's parking lot."

"Alright, look, when we get round there, take everything you want out of it."

"Okay, but what you gon do with it?"

"I'm gon leave it somewhere," Curt said before pulling away from the curb, and after quickly driving around the block, he pulled up in the student's parking lot.

"My car's on the second aisle," Tamaya said nervously.

"Alright, well once we get to it, hurry up and get what you gon get cause we to get out of here," Curt replied while suddenly coming to a stop behind her car.

Quickly hopping out, Tamaya opened her car door and began removing items from the glove compartment. After throwing the items into the backseat of Curt's car, she opened her truck and began looking around for the things she wanted to take with her.

"Damn, you ain't finished yet?"

"Almost, but I want to know what you gon do with my

car."

"I'm thinking bout leaving it in Overtown."

"In Overtown! If you leave it there, somebody's gon steal it."

"That's right, and if the police catch 'em in it, maybe they'll think that they're the ones robbing the banks.

"Okay, but what about me? I mean, they gon still want to talk to me right?"

"Probably, that's why we gon go somewhere and get a room. At least until we can figure out what we gon do."

"Alright, but I need to go by my apartment to get some clothes."

"I got you," Curt replied. "But right now, let's drop the car off and find a room. We'll go by there when it gets dark."

"And what if the police are already there?"

"Then you can buy some."

"Alright, well let's get out of here," Tamaya said before closing the trunk, and as Curt climbed behind the wheel of her car and started it up, she jumped in the car with Snag.

"You talked to Crystal?" he asked as they drove out of the parking lot.

"Yeah, she's good. I mean, I told her what happened and I told her that she ain't had nothing to worry about. At least not right now."

"Yeah, well, we gotta figure out what we gon do and we need to do it quick cause I can't afford to lose my job," Tamaya replied as they made a right on 20th Street and 3rd Avenue and headed south. Then suddenly coming up on Town Park, Snag pulled over behind Curt on the side of the road. As Snag and Tamaya looked on, Curt got out and walked back to his car, and after climbing in, Snag pulled off.

***

"Alright, we got the work back so now what?" Blue asked as he stood with Craig in Craig's kitchen.

"Well, I doubt we gon get the money back so we might as well concentrate on getting rid of that shit," Craig replied.

"Okay, but what about the nigga, Trigga? Cause you know he gon want some get back from that shit with Ray Ray.

"Yeah, I've been thinkin bout that and we gon have to be on point when we're handling our business."

"I feel you, but why we just don't go over to the Diamonds and get it over with?"

"Cause like I told you before, if we go over there and something happens, the police gon be looking at us like we wrong."

"Yeah, but at the same time, he won't be expecting us to come over there."

"No, but the police are probably still ridin round looking for the ma'fuckas who murked Ray Ray last night. Now if you want to go out there and risk getting caught with the gun we used, that's on you, but I'm staying right here and if that nigga brings his ass round here, it's on."

"Well, eventually we gon run down on his ass anyway."

"Yeah, but in the meantime, we might as well get some money."

"Alright so what, we gon cook all this shit up?"

"Just the half a key for right now. That way, all we'll have to worry about is getting rid of it."

"Yeah, I'm feelin that but what's up with that bitch Tamaya?" Blue suddenly asked.

"What you mean, what's up with her?"

"Well, I ain't seen her or her friend since I saw them with them niggas Curt and Snag."

"Shit, come to think, I ain't seen them niggas either."

"Nigga, with all the other shit that's been goin on, them ma'fuckers the last thing on my mind."

"Oh, so you saying that you ain't trying to fuck with her no more?"

"Nah, I'm just sayin that I got more important things to worry about."

"Yeah, whatever nigga, you just talkin."

"Look, we lost eighty grand and that ain't no lil bit of money."

"Hell, nah!"

"And what I'm trying to tell you is that chasin behind a bitch ain't gon bring it back. Now let's get this cooked up so we can open up shop."

"Yeah, alright," Blue replied, and while cutting open one of the packages, Craig wondered to himself just what Tamaya was up to.

CHAPTER 37

"Listen, detective, I don't need you coming in here tryin' to tell me how to do my job," the Department of Motor Vehicles Supervisor said while facing Detective Nelson and Officer Chambers.

"Alright, now you listen to me," Detective Nelson replied. "I have a court order signed by a Judge Miller ordering you to cooperate with the investigation and in furtherance of that, you are to give me whatever assistance I need in regards to the list of names I have. Oh, and may I remind you that if you refuse to cooperate, I can have you brought up on charges of obstruction."

"Are you married, detective?" The supervisor suddenly asked.

"No, but what does that have to do with anything?"

"Nothing, but I can see why no one would marry you."

"Now wait a minute! What's that supposed to mean?"

"It means that if you don't change, you're gonna spend a lot of lonely nights taking cold showers."

"Hold on now, what are you some kind of relationship expert or something? Cause I don't see no ring on your finger."

"Well, for your information, I was married to a cop for thirty years and like you, he was bossy, but over the years, I learned how to deal with him."

"Yeah, and how was that?"

"I ignored him," she replied with a smirk. "You see, detective, when dealing with a woman, you have to learn to be versatile. You have to know when to be pushy and forceful and when to use finesse. With your colleagues, being pushy may work, but in case you haven't noticed, I'm not one of them and being pushy definitely doesn't work on me."

"Okay, if I was being pushy, I'm sorry," Detective Nelson said as Officer Chambers snickered behind him. "But you've got to understand that this is a very serious matter."

"And so is my job, detective. I'm entrusted with some very sensitive information and I take protecting it very seriously. Now, let's start over, how may I help you?"

"We have a list of names that I need addressed for."

"Alright, I can do that. You have the names?"

"Yeah, right here," Detective Nelson said while removing the piece of paper with the names on it from his pocket, and as he handed it to her, an idea suddenly hit him. "Hey, is it possible for you to tell me if any of those people have a car registered to them?"

"Sure, anything else?"

"No, that's all for now."

"Alright, just give me a minute," the supervisor said as

she began typing on the computer and minutes later, the first name on the list appeared on the screen.

"Okay, you have a Coreen Johnson age 47 and there's a 2008 Nissan Altima registered to her."

"Nah, everything's all wrong, do you have picture of her?"

"Yeah, right here. See for yourself," she said while turning the computer to face him.

"Okay, that's not her."

"Alright, the next one is Cathy Adkins," the supervisor said while tapping the keys and seconds later, her face appeared on the screen.

"No, that's not her either."

"Alright, moving on," and typing in the next name, they waited for the computer to respond.

"Okay, we got a Lashawn Scott and—"

"It's not her," Detective Nelson said cutting her off.

"Alright, who's next on the list?"

"Tamaya Taylor."

"Now, let's see if she's who you're looking for," the supervisor said while typing her name into the computer. Seconds later, her face filled the screen.

"Hey, that's her," Detective Nelson said while leaning in for a closer look. Does she have a car registered to her?"

"Yeah, it's an uh! Here it is, a 2010 Toyota Camry."

"What about color?"

"Right here it says red, but with people painting their cars the way they're doing now, who knows."

"Yeah, well, you think I can get a copy of that?"

"Sure, if you say the magic word."

"Please!"

"That's better, and Detective, there's hope for you yet," she said with a smirk before hitting the print button on her computer. As they waited in silence, the printer buzzed and out popped the printout.

"Here you go, detective."

"Thank you so much."

"Don't mention it. You just remember what I said."

"Oh, I will," he replied before rushing out of the office with Officer Chambers right on his heels, and while making their way back to the car, he looked up to see Officer Chambers smiling.

"What?"

"I've never seen anyone put you in your place before."

"Look, if you tell anyone, I'll shoot you myself," Detective Nelson said as they approached the car.

"Trust me, you don't have to worry about me saying a word."

"Good, now let's go pay Ms. Taylor a visit," he shot back and after climbing into the car he started it up, put it in gear, and drove off.

***

"Boy, now I know you're crazy! Tamaya screamed while standing in the hotel room with Curt.

"Nah, I mean, think about it. Ain't no way they gon expect for us to hit another bank now. Besides, how else we gon get the money we need?"

"Look, I feel you, but I just don't know."

"You just don't know what? 'Cause just this morning you

was down for whatever."

"Yeah, but that was before I found out that they was looking for me."

"Okay, but they gon be looking for you regardless."

"True, but suppose something goes wrong while we're in the bank?"

"Something like what?"

"I don't know, but look what happened to y'all last time."

"That was just a coincidence. Why you think I was stressin bout you practicing? Two minutes, Tamaya, that's all we need and we'll have over two hundred grand. Add that to what we already have and we'll be able to go somewhere and chill for a while."

"I hear what you're saying, but what about all the other stuff?"

"What other stuff?"

"Me just up and quitting my job, and then what about my car?"

"Well, if anything happens to your car, the insurance will pay for it, so you good. Now as for your job, what else you gon do? I mean, you can keep your job and pray they don't come."

"Yeah, right, you know damn well they gon come eventually."

"Yeah, but you can tell 'em you don't know nothing."

"Like they gon believe me."

"So, you really ain't got no choice. Well, you do, but you already know how that's gon play out."

"Yeah, and believe me, I ain't tryin to go to jail."

"Shit, I ain't tryin to let you go," Curt said with a smile.

"If that happened, I couldn't get no more of this," he continued while slipping his hand under her skirt.

"Boy, stop! We got all the police in Miami looking for us and all you can think about is some pussy?"

"What else I'm supposed to be thinking bout? I mean, it is what it is and ain't nothing we can say or do to change it."

"Alright look, if I decide to go ahead and do this with you, when were you planning to do it?"

"Well, today's Tuesday, so if we do it Friday, will you be ready?"

"Yeah, if you are."

"Shit, I could do it today."

"You know what I mean."

"Yeah," and before he could say another word, he was interrupted by the sound of someone knocking at the door.

"Who's that?" Tamaya asked nervously.

"It's probably Snag," Curt replied before looking through he peephole, and spotting Snag on the other side of the door, he quickly opened it.

"What's up?"

"Shit, I came over here to ask y'all," Snag said before stepping into the room.

"Well, we were just talking and we figured we'd go by the apartment to pick up some clothes then come back here."

"Alright, then what?"

"Then we can take our time figuring out what we gon do next."

"Well, we need to come up with something, cause if we stay in Miami for too long, them crackas gon have our ass under the jail."

"Look, let's just go. Then we'll pick up something to eat before coming back here to brainstorm a lil bit."

"That'll work, and I'll meet y'all downstairs," Snag replied before opening the door and walking out. As Curt and Tamaya followed him out, Curt was already trying to figure out what bank they would hit.

CHAPTER 38

"Damn, this shit's jumpin," Craig said as he watched another customer drive by.

"Yeah, but with all these cars coming through here, we better be on point cause that nigga Trigga just might decide to ride through here."

"Man, fuck that nigga. You act like we scared of him or something."

"Nah, I'm just saying we need to be on point cause with all these cars, ain't no telling who's who, you feel me?"

"Yeah, but I still think we should've went over there and took care of that."

"And like I told you, we gotta act like we in the right."

"I hear you, but at the same time..." and suddenly spotting Blue staring at something, he turned to see what he was looking at and spotted a car with dark tints creeping.

"You see that?"

"Damn right, but keep an eye on the hallway," Blue replied while pulling out his pistol and quickly chambering a round, he ducked down next to the car closest to him.

Meanwhile, after pulling out his gun and flipping the safety off, Craig kept his eyes glued to the hallway and remembering how Trigga snuck up on 'em before, he refused to fall for it a second time.

Creeping along, the car headed in their direction. As they both looked on, it came to a stop directly in front of them.

"Can you see who's driving?"

"Nah, the tints are too dark," and as soon as the words left his mouth, the car door opened.

"Hey, y'all the one who got the fifty pieces." A middle aged white man asked.

"Yeah, why what's up?"

"I want six of 'em if they fat."

"Oh, they fat," Craig replied while breathing a sigh of relief, and tucking his gun back in his pants, he pulled out his stash to serve the latest customer.

Still on point, Blue watched closely as the man walked back to his car, got in, and drove off.

"Man, out here with the bullshit, got me all paranoid," Craig said smiling, and just as he folded the money and stuffed it in his pocket, the windows of the car next to him exploded.

"What the fuck!" He screamed while diving on the ground. Peeking around the bumper of the car, he spotted Trigga hanging out of a car window firing an AK in their direction.

"That's that nigga, Trigga!" He screamed.

"Yeah, I know," Blue replied as shattered glass rained down on them, and as Trigga continued firing round after round in their direction, they couldn't get a shot off.

The Glock .40 pistols they carried were no match for the AK Trigga had, but suddenly spotting an opening as the car drove by, they both jumped up and began firing in the car's direction. Round after round hit the car knocking out the back glass, and suddenly spotting Trigga aim his gun in their direction, they ducked behind another car the moment he pulled the trigger.

"Fuck!" Craig screamed as the bullets passed close enough to them to feel their heat and just as it suddenly began, it was over as Trigga's car sped out the gate. Looking around at all the bullet riddled cars, they both wondered how they'd survived and hearing the sirens in the distance, they knew it wouldn't be long before the parking lot was swarming with police.

"We gotta get out of here."

"Yeah, but where we gon go?"

"Anywhere but here," Blue said while fumbling with his keys. After finally getting the car door open, he climbed behind the wheel. Starting it up, he waited for Craig to climb in. The moment the door closed behind him, Blue sped off without hesitation.

***

"Attention all units! We have a report of shots fired in the apartment complex on 103rd Street and 17th Avenue."

"Hey, ain't that where we're headed?" Officer Chambers suddenly asked while listening to the radio transmission.

"Yeah, it is," Detective Nelson replied while placing the

flashing light on top of his car."

"You think it has something to do with."

"Son of a bitch!"

"What?"

"Ain't that the car we're looking for?"

"Where?"

"Right there," Officer Chambers said pointing.

"Yeah, that's it, and there's two black males inside."

"Yeah, so you think—"

"Put on your seatbelt." Detective Nelson said cutting him off, and suddenly stepping on the gas, he gave chase, "Call in our position."

"I'm already on it," Officer Chamber said before speaking into the mic. "Attention all available units, this is Officer Chambers and I along with Detective Nelson are in pursuit of a red Toyota Camry carrying two black male suspects possibly involved in the deaths of two police officers. Be advised that these suspects may also be responsible for robbing several banks and are considered armed and extremely dangerous. We're traveling north on 7th Avenue approaching the Golden Glades Interchange. Any units heading in this direction be advised that we'd like to keep the suspects from getting onto Interstate 95."

"Too late," Detective Nelson replied while weaving in and out of traffic. Minutes later, they headed onto Interstate 95 at a high rate of speed.

"Looks like we're on our own on this one."

"Well, if that's the case, let's do it," Officer Chambers replied, and as the speed reached upwards of a hundred miles an hour, he held on for dear life.

Detective Nelson had been involved in several high speed chases and he'd seen them end badly. If the men up ahead were in fact the men who killed the two officers, God help them because he wasn't about to let them get away. With speeds in excess of a hundred miles an hour, the two cars raced in and out of traffic as shocked motorists looked on, and while approaching the 62nd Street exit, the Toyota suddenly veered across four lanes of traffic in an attempt to exit the interstate.

"They'll never make it!" Officer Chambers screamed as the car braked hard while trying to maneuver through traffic. As it suddenly sideswiped a Dodge Caravan, he looked on in horror as the car slammed head on into an Isuzu Rodeo.

"Oh, my God!" Officer Chambers screamed as the car seemed to disintegrate right before his eyes, and as Detective Nelson suddenly pulled the car to a stop, they jumped out to see bodies lying everywhere.

"I've got a visual on one of the suspects," Detective Nelson said before rushing over to where he lay.

"I see the other one," Officer Chambers replied, "But he's not moving."

"Secure him anyway, helps on the way."

"Alright," and as he obeyed the commands, he looked to his left to see the driver of the Isuzu staring up at him with wide eyes.

"Just hold on, help's on the way," he said while handcuffing the suspect's hands behind his back.

"I can't feel my legs," the woman replied weakly.

"We'll get you to the hospital and they'll get you fixed up," he shot back in an attempt to comfort her, and looking around at the carnage, he wondered if it was even possible.

"How is she?"

"She's alert, said something about not being able to feel her legs," Officer Chambers replied as the sounds of sirens grew louder.

"Yeah, well, there's not much that can be done for her until the paramedics arrive."

"Okay, but you think these are our guys?"

"If they are, the question now is where's the girl."

***

"Fuck! I knew I should've got out and handled my business," Trigga said while pacing back and forth inside his apartment. "Now them ma'fuckers know I'm on their trail."

"Man, don't even worry about it. We'll run down on 'em sooner or later."

"Nigga, I ain't on that later shit. I want them niggas dead now and I ain't gon rest till they is."

"Yeah, well, I need to find somewhere to park my car cause the last thing I need is for the police to see it all shot up."

"I'm going back tonight."

"What?"

"I said, I'm going back tonight."

"Man, you know how many police gon be lurking round there?"

"I don't give a fuck, and if they get in the way they can get it, too."

"Man, listen—"

"Nah, nigga you listen," Trigga said cutting him off. "Them niggas had something to do with Ray Ray getting killed and I ain't gon shit, shave, or bathe til they dead, too. Now if you don't want nothing to do with it, I respect that, but man, I'm all in," and suddenly remembering Ray Ray slumped over in his bullet riddled car, he promised not to let it happen again.

CHAPTER 39

"Alright, y'all listen up. We ain't got to be bullshittin so once we get there, get what y'all gon—oh shit! Look," Curt screamed after seeing the parking lot swarming with police.

"Man, what the—"

"Keep going," Snag said.

"Shit, you ain't gotta tell me twice, but where all the ma'fuckers come from?"

"They looking for us, that's what they doin' round there," Tamaya suddenly said from the backseat.

"That's a lot of damn police to just be lookin for us."

"You must've forgot about the two police who got killed. Oh, yeah, and they probably got labeled as armed and dangerous."

"It wouldn't surprise me."

"No, but now what? Better yet, pull over right here."

"Right where?"

"Right there by the store," Snag said pointing.

"Alright, but what's over there?" Curt asked while pulling up in the parking lot.

"I'm gon try to find out what happened. Hey, that's that nigga Troy right there," and as soon as Curt parked, Snag jumped out the car and headed for Troy.

"They're probably in my apartment right now," Tamaya said in frustration.

"Look, just chill til we find out what goin on."

"Just chill! The parking lot of our apartment building is full of police and you tell me to chill?"

"Yeah, cause they might not even be at your apartment."

"So, what they doin there, huh? Tell me that?"

"I don't know, but I'm sure Snag gon be able to tell us something when he finish tellin to whoever he's talking to."

"Alright, but he needs to hurry," Tamaya replied and a few minutes later, Snag came walking back to the car.

"Man, them crackas round there cause they say somebody tried to rob that nigga, Craig," he said while climbing back in the car.

"Somebody tried to rob Craig?"

"Yeah, and I don't know what happened but they ended up in a shootout and a lot of cars got shot up."

"Did they catch whoever did it?"

"Nah, they say whoever it was got away."

"What about Craig?"

"Don't nobody know where he at."

"And we sittin here thinking that they over there looking for us," Curt said smiling.

"Shit, how else we supposed to think? I mean, all this shit gotta bitch paranoid."

"Yeah, I feel you cause when I first saw all them ma'fuckas, I didn't know what to think either."

"Crystal gon probably have a heart attack when she gets home and sees 'em."

"Nah, cause I'm gon call her and tell her what's up. Ain't no need to have her scared for nothing."

"True, but now what we gon do cause ain't no telling how long them ma'fuckers gon be over there."

"Hold up! I know you ain't scared."

"Nah, but I ain't stupid either. Why go round there with all them ma'fuckers running round all over the place when I can wait till they leave?"

"I know that's right, but now what?"

"Well, I'm hungry," Tamaya suddenly said.

"Alright, well let's go get something to eat. Then, we'll come back and see if we can get in to grab some clothes."

"And what if we can't?"

"Then we'll come back once they leave."

"It sounds good to me," Snag said. As Curt backed out of the parking lot and drove off, he sat in the backseat wondering how they'd gotten themselves into the mess that they were in.

***

"So, you want to tell me what happened?" The lieutenant asked while standing with Detective Nelson and Officer Chambers.

"Well, while investigating the bank robberies, one of which resulted in the deaths of two police officers, we received information about a potential witness. As we were on our way to talk to this individual, we saw the car."

"What was it doing?"

"Just sitting in traffic."

"Okay, go on."

"At the same time, a call came out over the radio about a shooting inside the same apartment complex where the potential witness lives and because of that, I placed my blue light on the top of the car."

"So, did the call come across the radio before you noticed the car or afterwards?"

"Before."

"So, in other words, you had already placed your light on top of the car, and then you spotted the car."

"That's correct. When I attempted to pull the car over, a chase ensued onto Interstate 95 ending up here."

"Now, you understand that there's a protocol in place for engaging in car chases? Especially where innocent people are put in danger."

"Yes, sir, and we had every reason to stop the vehicle. Not only is it the car that was seen on the bank's surveillance camera, but witnesses also described the suspects as two African American males."

"So, you had probable cause which is important because at the inquiry, they'll want to know if that was the case. So far so good, because in pursuit of murder suspects, you're allowed a lot of leeway. Now, I have to get back to the office because the chief wants to give a news conference, but I expect your report on my desk by sixteen hundred hours."

"It will be, sir," Detective Nelson replied before watching him the lieutenant turn and walk away.

"We're out here trying to catch the bad guys and all he's

concerned about is did we follow proper procedure," Officer Chambers said.

"Yeah, all they care about is covering their asses. Anyway, did any of the suspects regain consciousness?"

"No, but I took their fingerprints and sent them to the lab for comparison."

"Good job, but something's bothering me," Detective Nelson said.

"What?"

"Why would two bank robbers, not to mention cop killers, be riding around in a car that belongs to a customer who was inside a bank during the robbery? They have to know that we'd review the surveillance tape. It just doesn't make sense. I mean, we found the getaway car still in the parking lot so where do the women fit in?"

"That's what we're trying to find out," Officer Chambers replied.

"Yeah, it is, and it won't hurt to talk to our two suspects as soon as they wake up."

"What a wakeup call that would be, huh?"

"Yeah," Detective Nelson replied as they headed to the back of the car, and after climbing in and starting it up, he put it in gear and headed to the hospital.

***

"Okay, now what?" Craig asked as they sat at the light on 95th Street and 17th Avenue.

"Well, we definitely can't go back to the apartments cause by now, the police are all round that ma'fucker."

"Yeah, and I can't believe that nigga came round here again with the bullshit."

"I can cause that's what I would've done," Blue replied. "Matter of fact, go by the Diamonds."

"What?"

"I said—"

"Oh, I heard what you said," Craig said cutting him off, "But I'm trying to figure out why?"

"Because the last thing he gon expect is for us to come round there right now."

"Yeah, but we left the choppa in the apartment."

"So what, we got these," Blue said while holding up his Glock. After putting in a fresh clip, Craig made a left and headed towards 7th Avenue.

"We gon come up in the back so make a left on 8th Avenue," Blue said before chambering a round. "I'm gon get out and walk up the street while you drive by."

"What if you see one of 'em?"

"I'm gon handle my business. You just be ready to move once I get back to the car."

"Man, I don't know. Don't you think it'll be better if both of us got out?"

"Look, somebody needs to stay with the car just in case we have to hurry up and get out of here."

"Alright, but man, watch yourself cause you already know that nigga ain't scared to shoot."

"Me either," Blue replied as Craig suddenly made a left. While heading towards the Diamonds, he thought about what lay ahead.

Finally reaching 101st Street, Craig made a right and

suddenly spotted the car they'd seen earlier pulling out of the parking lot.

"Hey, ain't that the car Trigga was just in?"

"Yeah, that's it."

"Well, he ain't in it now."

"No, but the nigga who was with him is."

"So, what you gon do?"

"Block it off."

"What?"

"Nigga, block the car off," Blue repeated and as the car slowly headed in their direction, Craig suddenly veered left blocking the car's path.

Blue quickly threw the door open, and before the driver of the other car could react, he jumped out firing.

Caught slipping, Chevy ducked as the rounds shattered the driver's side window, and looking up in shock, he came face to face with Blue just as the fired several rounds into him.

Snatching the car door open, Blue grabbed him by the collar and as his body fell out, Blue fired two more shots into the side of his head. Spotting the bag of money on the front seat, Blue grabbed it before rushing back to the car. As the residents of the complex began coming out of their apartments, Craig sped off in a cloud of dust.

CHAPTER 40

Hearing the shots, Trigga immediately thought about Chevy, and after running back to his room to grab his gun, he ran outside and began looking around frantically. Spotting a crowd forming down the street, he took off at a dead run. After finally approaching, he pushed his way through the crowd only to have his worst fears realized. There on the ground next to his car was Chevy staring up at the sky. One side of his head was blown away, and the blood stained the pavement around his body.

Looking around at the faces in the crowd, Trigga had murder in his eyes, and having seen that same look many times, people in the crowd began backing away slowly.

"Anybody see who did this?" Trigga asked as sirens could be heard in the distance.

"Yeah, it was two niggas in a grey Chevy," someone replied.

"Was one of 'em a red nigga with dreads?"

"Yeah."

"Damn!" Trigga screamed as he thought of Craig and Blue coming around there suddenly hit him, and knowing that the only way this was going to end was if one of them was dead. He stood and headed back to his apartment. Getting a car was the first order of business. Then, he'd set out to find them both and when he did, somebody was going to die.

***

"So, have you figured out which bank we gon hit?" Tamaya asked while sitting in the restaurant with Curt.

"Yeah."

"So, do you plan on telling me?"

"Yeah, but you need to hold that down cause Snag don't know about what we're planning.

"Why? I mean, I thought he was your friend."

"He is."

"So why you didn't tell him?"

"Look, do you tell Crystal everything you do?"

"No."

"Why, ain't she your friend?"

"Yeah, but oh—I see what you're saying."

"Alright then, now listen up. We gon hit The Bank of America on 54th Street and 27th Avenue."

"Okay, but why that one?"

"Because it's not too far out of the way. Plus, I know my way round the area."

"Yeah, alright, so when we gon go scope it out?"

"Maybe tomorrow, or if you want, we can go tonight after

we grab some clothes and drop Snag off back at the hotel."

"Have you decided where you gon steal the car from?"

"Shit, we can steal a car from anywhere and once I do, I can park it either in the flat tops on 53rd Street or in Clown City on 64th across from the Metro Rail Station. Both of 'em are close enough so that we won't have to drive too far. Plus, if something crazy happens, I know a couple of people round there."

"Okay, well once we do this, we need to go somewhere cause—"

"Hey! Y'all bout ready to go?" Snag suddenly asked interrupting them.

"Yeah, all we need is the check," Curt replied.

"Well, I'll take care of that. Y'all just come on," Snag shot back before walking off to go pay the tab. As soon as they were alone again, Tamaya resumed their conversation.

"So, like I was sayin, once we handle our business, we need to go somewhere because I ain't tryin to go to jail."

"Yeah, I hear you."

"Curt, I'm serious."

"Shit, I'm serious, too."

"Well, alright so—"

"Damn! Y'all coming or what?" Snag screamed cutting her off, and after leaving a generous tip, Curt headed for the door with Tamaya right on his heels.

"Man, what's wrong with y'all?" Snag asked as soon as they were outside.

"Nothing, why?"

"Cause, I'm tryin to get out of here and y'all round here bullshittin."

"Man, look."

"Nah, nigga you look. Just cause them crackas been dealin with all the other shit that's been gon on, don't mean that they forgot about us."

"Oh, I know that."

"Well, you need to act like it."

"Man, I got this, alright? Now let's go back by the apartments to see if they still there."

"And what if they is?"

"Then we'll just come back later," Curt replied as they finally made it to the car. After jumping in and starting it up, he put it in gear and drove off.

***

Finally arriving at Jackson Memorial Hospital, Detective Nelson parked his county issued sedan before climbing out and heading inside. With Officer Chambers right behind him, the two men walked up the front desk and identified themselves to the receptionist.

"Excuse me, my name is Detective Nelson from The City of Miami Police Department and I'd like to inquire about two accident victims who just came in."

"I'm sorry, but we can't give out that kind of information."

"Alright, let me speak to your supervisor."

Why? Cause she gon tell you the same thing I just told you."

"Okay, now you listen to me," Detective Nelson said through gritted teeth. "I've got two dead police officers and the men suspected of killing them were just brought in. Now, either you tell me what I want to know or I'll have you arrested."

"For what?"

"Obstruction of justice, and if you think I'm bluffing, try me."

"Alright, what did you say your name was?"

"Listen, they're African American males, maybe mid-twenties and they just came in."

"Two patients fitting that description are being held in the jail wing. You can go through those double doors right there," and she never got to finish her sentence because both Detective Nelson and Officer Chambers had already walked off.

"Come on, this way," Detective Nelson said as they approached another receptionist.

"May I help you?" she asked as they walked up.

"Yes, we're looking for the two accident victims who were just brought in."

"You mean the two black boys, right?"

"Ah, yeah, that's them."

"Well, one of 'em is still unconscious and the other one is being prepped for surgery."

"Prepped for surgery!"

"Yeah, he has a broken pelvis, a dislocated shoulder, and a host of other injuries."

"Well, is it possible for me to talk to him before he goes into surgery."

"You'll have to talk to the doctor about that."

"And who's he?"

"Doctor Simms."

"Is there any way for me to speak to him?"

"Yeah, you're in luck cause he's right there."

"Where?"

"Right there." The receptionist said pointing. Turning in the direction she was pointing, he spotted the doctor.

"Excuse me, sir," he said rushing over. "I'm Detective Nelson from The City of Miami Police Department and you have a suspect in a police shooting about to go into surgery and I need to speak to him."

"Did you say a suspect in a police shooting?"

"Actually two police officers were killed, but yeah."

"Well, detective, I don't normally do this, but under the circumstances, I'll make an exception. You got five minutes. He's in the third room on your right."

"Thank you, doctor," Detective Nelson replied before rushing off, and with Officer Chambers right behind him, he walked into the room to see a young man lying on a gurney.

"Who are you?" he asked.

"The person who's gonna save your life." Detective Nelson replied.

"What?"

"The car you were driving, where'd you get it?"

"None of your business."

"Well, you better make it my business because that car was involved in a bank robbery where two police officers were killed. Now if you—"

"Hold up!" the man said cutting him off. "I don't know nothing about no robbery."

"Well, you'd better make me believe you."

“Alright look, me and my friend saw the car parked by Town Park so we took it.”

“Why’d you speed off?”

“Because I didn’t want to go to jail for stealing it.”

“So, you don’t know someone name Tamaya Taylor?”

“Who’s that?”

“She’s the owner of the car you stole.”

“Like I said, we saw the car on the Park so we took it. I don’t know nothin bout no bank robbery, no police getting killed, and I definitely don’t know nobody name whatever you just said.

“Alright, then listen—”

“Times up, detective,” the doctor said cutting him off.

“Just one more minute, doc.”

“I just gave you five. Now, if you’ll excuse me, I also have a job to do.”

“Okay,” Detective Nelson replied, and as he headed for the door, he turned his attention back to the man on the bed.

“If I find out you’re lying, I’ll make sure you die in prison.”

“Get out, detective!” the doctor said while pushing him out of the room. As the door closed behind him, Officer Chambers turned to face him.

“So, do you believe him.”

“Yeah, unfortunately I do.”

“Alright, so now what?

“We go find the girl.”

CHAPTER 41

"Alright, turn right here," Blue said while looking behind them to make sure they weren't being followed.

"Okay, now what?"

"Slow down, cause you go pull up in the yard of the Blue and white house coming up on your left."

"Right there?"

"Yeah, that's it, pull round back."

"Alright, but whose house is this?"

"A friend of mine."

"He ain't gon say nothin bout us parking here?"

"Man, look, you think I'd tell you to park here if he was gon say something?"

"Nah."

"Alright, now hurry up cause we got other shit to do."

"Yeah, I hear you, but what's that?"

"Some money that nigga had on the front seat."

"Well, damn nigga, bust the bag and see how much it is," Craig said while pulling the car around the back of the house and after parking, he cut the engine off and waited as Blue pulled the money out of the bag.

"So, what you think? Do those look like ten grand stacks?"

"Yeah, bout that."

"So, five of 'em is fifty grand."

"Shit, that's fifty grand of our money back."

"It's fifty grand, but it ain't our money."

"Huh?"

"I mean, it's ours now but it ain't the money they took from us."

"How you know?"

"Cause we didn't have all one hundred dollar bills."

"Alright, but where you think they got it from?" Craig asked after thinking about the recent bank robberies.

"It really don't matter to me cause fifty grand is fifty grand."

"Yeah, I feel you, but now what? Cause I just know that somebody round there saw my car."

"That's why I told you to park it back here. We can leave it here, at least til the heat dies down."

"Alright, but now how we gon get round?"

"We can use my car, but we gon have to be careful cause Trigga's gon definitely be looking for us."

"Yeah, well, he better be looking for us cause we gon be looking for his ass, too."

"Damn right! But the only problem now is we don't know what kind of car he's driving."

"Yeah, but he don't know what kind of car we driving either," Blue replied.

"Alright, but what we gon do now? Cause the police hon

be round there for a minute."

"True, and that means that Trigga ain't gon be able to move like he wants to til they do."

"Which means?"

"That we got time to put together a plan. Now, come on."

***

"Damn, them ma'fuckers still there." Craig said as they drove past the apartments.

"Yeah, and ain't no tellin how long they gon be there." Curt replied.

"Well, we need to do something cause I need some clothes," Tamaya whined. "Especially if we gon be stayin in a hotel for a couple of days."

"Well, we can stop and grab some clothes right quick."

"Nigga, is you crazy! Ain't no way I'm going round there with all them crackas up in there."

"Why? I mean, they ain't round there lookin for us."

"No, but still."

"But still what?"

"But they still round there, that what."

"Look, we can park by the Popeyes Chicken Restaurant and walk back to the apartments. Then, we grab some clothes and whatever else we gon take and get out of there."

"And what if somebody recognizes us, or Tamaya?"

"Okay, she can stay in the car and we can got to her apartment for her."

"No, I'm going," Tamaya suddenly said as Snag made a right on 17th Avenue before pulling up in the Popeyes

Chicken Restaurant parking lot.

"Alright look, we ain't got all day to be sittin here arguing about who gon go and who ain't. Let's just go ahead and get what we gon get and get out of there before them ma'fuckers do come looking for us."

"Alright then, everybody meet back here in ten minutes," Snag said.

"How y'all expect me to get my stuff."

"Ten minutes," Snag said cutting her off. "The last thing we need is to get caught in the house."

"Yeah, alright, ten minutes," Tamaya said while climbing out of the car. As soon as everyone had gotten out, they all headed for the apartments.

Walking with an air of confidence, Curt and Snag ignored the activity going on around them and headed straight for Curt's apartment. After sliding the key in the lock and unlocking the door, they both stepped inside before closing the door behind them.

Meanwhile, Tamaya was sweating bullets as she headed upstairs to her apartment. With every step, she imagined that someone was watching her. *I should've stayed my ass in the car,* she said to herself while finally making it to the top of the stairs. Suddenly spotting two police officers standing four doors down from her apartment, she pulled out her keys and rushed inside. After quickly calming her nerves, she rushed into her room and went straight for her closet.

Grabbing a bag, she began stuffing it with clothes, and while sorting through them, she wondered what would happen to the stuff she left behind. *Four or five outfits should be enough,* she said to herself while searching through her wardrobe, and after choosing a couple of low maintenance outfits, she grabbed some shoes to match. Rushing into the bathroom, she grabbed her toothbrush and other feminine products before walking over to her dresser and snatching open her underwear drawer.

After stuffing a couple of pairs in her bag, she walked out into the kitchen for a cold glass of water. Throwing her bag over her shoulder, she headed for the door. Peeking out to make sure the coast was clear, she stepped out, and after closing and locking the door behind her, she began walking back to the car. Minutes later, she reached the car to find Curt and Snag waiting for her, and after climbing in the backseat, Snag pulled off at the same time that Detective Nelson was pulling into the parking lot of the apartment complex.

***

"So, what made you believe him?" Officer Chambers asked as Detective Chambers turned into the parking lot.

"Huh?"

"The boy back at the hospital, what made you believe him?"

"Because things just didn't add up. I mean, think about it. If you had just robbed a bank and killed two police officers, would you be riding around with no guns?"

"No."

"Why?"

"Because for one, I'd know the police were looking for me."

"What's the other reason?"

"Before I'd die in prison. I'd hold court in the streets."

"My point exactly. And neither of them had a gun. They didn't even have money in their pockets. They found a car parked on the side of the road and stole it to go joyriding."

"It won't be the last time that happened."

"No, now what apartment are we looking for?"

"222."

"Okay, let's go," Detective Nelson said while climbing out of the car, and as they both headed for the stairs, they noticed a lot of activity around them.

"Are they still investigating that shooting from earlier?"

"It appears so," Officer Chambers replied as they made it to the top of the stairs. Searching for apartment 222, they spotted two officers heading in their direction.

"Hey, detective, what brings you around here?" one of them asked.

"I'm conducting an investigation unrelated to what's going on here."

"Yeah, well somebody shot up the parking lot pretty good."

"I heard, anybody get hit?"

"Nah, just a lot of property damage. So, what y'all looking for?"

"A woman by the name of Tamaya Taylor. She lives in apartment 222."

"Well, we just saw a girl go in there not long ago."

"Is this her"? Detective Nelson asked while removing the picture from his pocket and showing it to them.

"Yeah, that's her."

"How long ago did you did you see her?"

"Not even ten minutes. Matter of fact, she just walked towards 17th Avenue carrying a bag or something."

"You sure?"

"I'm positive, we just saw her."

"Come on," Detective Nelson said before trotting in that direction. By the time Officer Chambers caught up with him in the parking lot of the Popeyes Chicken Restaurant, Tamaya was long gone.

CHAPTER 42

"Hey, did y'all call Crystal to tell her what time it is?" Snag asked suddenly while getting onto Interstate 95.

"Yeah, I called her," Tamaya replied. "And I told her what hotel we stayin in so she'll be coming by when she gets off work."

"Shit, that'll work," Snag said with a smirk.

"I bet it will," Curt cut in. "At least you won't be up in the room all by yourself."

"Yeah, but at the same time, I think it's a good idea."

"Yeah, I mean it ain't like they're looking for her. Shit, for all we know, they don't even know about her."

"Look, it's me they want to talk to so she's good. We the ma'fuckers who should be worried." Curt replied as Snag exited the interstate and pulled up in the parking lot of the Days Inn Hotel on 79th Street and 6th Avenue.

"We gon be alright cause in a couple of days, we gon be so far away from Miami it ain't gon be funny."

"I hope you're right," Snag said while parking.

"Did Crystal say what time she was getting off?"

"Yeah, five o'clock, why?"

"Just asking. Now, I'm gon go up here to the room, take me a shower, and wait for her to come by."

"Yeah, well, we gon holla at y'all when we get back."

"Wait a minute! Where y'all going?"

"To holla at somebody right quick, why?"

"Cause y'all don't need to be out riding round especially with them crackas out there looking for us."

"Man, look, we gon be alright. Besides, we ain't gon be gone that long."

"Yeah, alright, but keep y'all phone on just in case I need to get in touch with y'all."

"Alright, we got you. Now, let us get out of here so we can hurry up and get back."

"Yeah, and on your way back, stop and get something to smoke." Snag replied before walking off. After watching him go, Curt drove out the parking lot.

"So, who you going to see?" Tamaya asked as he eased out into traffic.

"Nobody."

"But I thought you just told Snag that you were going to see somebody?"

"I did, but what else was I supposed to tell him? Oh, me and Tamaya goin to scope out the bank we planning to rob."

"No, but I still don't see why you keeping it from him."

"Cause he'd be totally against it and I couldn't blame him."

"So, hold up! You mean to tell me that you don't want to do this?"

"It ain't that, but at the same time, what choice we got? I

mean, we need the money and how else we supposed to get it?"

"Well, I don't know what you want me to tell you."

"Shit, I don't know what I want to hear." Curt replied as he drove through the intersection of 79th Street and 17th Avenue.

"Well, look let's do what we gotta do and we'll figure out what we gon do after that."

"Yeah, alright," Curt said, and minutes later, they made a left on 22nd Avenue. After reaching 54th Street, he made a right.

"When we get to 27th Avenue, I want you to pay attention. On your left, you gon have a store and the flat tops are right behind it. Down the street on 64th Street, you got Clown City. That's probably where I'll leave the car. That way, when we leave the bank, all we gotta do is make it up the street."

"Alright," Tamaya said while taking it all in, and as Curt suddenly made a left on 54th Street, he continued.

"We'll come from this way. Once I pull up in front of the bank, we go in, handle our business, and get out of there. It's as simple as that. Then, we can go back to the hotel and count our money."

"I know that's right," Tamaya said smiling. "But what's gon happen if the police get behind us?"

"You just put on your seatbelt and I'll handle the rest."

"Alright, I can do that."

"Good, now one more thing we need to take care of."

"What's that?"

"We need to find out how often the police ride past the bank," Curt replied as he drove down 27th Avenue. Suddenly making a U-turn, he drove back to the Church's Chicken Restaurant on the corner of 54th Street and 27th Avenue.

After turning up in the parking lot, he parked and headed inside with Tamaya right on his heels. After ordering something to drink, they found a seat by the window and waited.

***

"Come on, cuz, damn! You gon let me hold the car or what?" Trigga asked as he stood in his cousin's living room and tried to convince her to let him borrow her car.

"And what I'm gon drive if I have to go somewhere?"

"Damn, it ain't like I'm gon be gone all night."

"Mmm hmm! But that ain't the issue."

"So, what is?"

"What you gon do with it if I let you hold it?"

"Hold up! What you mean by that?"

"Boy, ain't nobody stupid. You act like nobody don't know what you be out there doing."

"Alright, look—"

"Nah, you look," his cousin said cutting him off. "If I let you hold it, what's in it for me?"

"What you want?"

"Shit, what you think I want? I mean, a bitch got bills to pay."

"So, in other words, you want to get broke off?"

"Damn right, and I saw your car on the news earlier. What happened?"

"Nothing."

"Boy, your car was all—"

"Look," Trigga said cutting her off. "How bout I give you ten grand."

"Boy, don't play."

"Nah, I'm serious. That way, if anything happens, you'll have enough money to get you another car."

"Alright, but where you gon get ten grand? That's what I want to know."

"Don't worry about it. All I want to know is if you good with that?"

"Hell, yeah!" she screamed, and without another word, Trigga removed the bag he had tucked in his pants. As his cousin looked on, he opened it and pulled out a wad of cash.

"Boy! Where?"

"I told you don't worry bout it," Trigga said cutting her off as he began counting out the money. Looking on in amazement, his cousin could barely contain her excitement.

Ten grand was a small price to pay for what he had in mind. Besides, he'd come up on almost three hundred thousand in a matter of days and the excitement he felt was nothing compared to what he'd feel after killing Craig and Blue. "Alright, that's ten grand. You good?"

"Damn right, but I still want to know where you got all that money from. And why you riding around with all that money on you."

"Look, just let me get the keys so I can get out of here," he said ignoring her question. As she walked off to retrieve them, he thought about what lay ahead.

"Here you go," she said while handing him the keys. "Now what time you gon bring my car back?"

"By morning."

"Alright now, don't let me have to come looking for your ass."

"Yeah, whatever. Anyway, I'm gon holla," he said before walking out. After climbing into his cousin's car and starting it up, he thought about his friends Ray Ray and Chevy. And after putting the car in gear, he headed for his apartment.

***

"So, let me get this straight, you want to set a trap for Trigga in the apartments?" Craig asked while sitting in traffic with Blue.

"Yeah."

"And how we gon do that? You seen all them ma'fuckas in the parking lot?"

"Yeah, I saw 'em, but they ain't go be there all night."

"No, but how you know Trigga gon come back?"

"Cause if I was him, I would," Blue replied. "Especially after what happened down the street from his apartment. That was the second person that be with him so I can just imagine what's going on in his head."

"Alright, so what's up with all that shit you was talking bout earlier?"

"Bout what?"

"You know, that shit bout us having the law on our side."

"Fuck that. Right now, it's about survival and if he brings his ass back round here, we gon give him the business."

"Alright, but tell me bout this trap shit you talkin bout."

"You remember how he came up in here the last time?"

"Yeah, what about it?"

"Well, this time when he comes, he ain't leaving. You see, one of us gon post up in a car by the front gate while the other waits in our usual spot. Once he pulls up in the parking lot, the one in the car by the front gate gone use it to block the exit. Then, he'll come round the side of the building and we'll handle our business."

"Hold up! What about the people tryin to leave?"

"Fuck 'em cause once that nigga brings his ass in the apartments, ain't nobody coming in or coming out."

"What about the police?"

"Shit, if we go ahead and handle our business, we should be long gone before they get there."

"Man, I don't know."

"You don't know what?"

"If that shit gon work."

"Why wouldn't it? I mean, the nigga comes, in we block him off, and handle our business. It's that simple," Blue said as they pulled up to the light on 151st Street and 7th Avenue.

"Alright, but then what?"

"Then, we go somewhere for few days, and once the heat dies down, we come back and get money like we always do."

"Yeah, alright," Craig replied, and as they made a left before pulling up in the parking lot of the McDonald's Restaurant, he had the odd feeling that it wasn't going to be that simple.

CHAPTER 43

"Okay, so now what?" Officer Chambers asked while standing in the middle of Tamaya's living room with Detective Nelson.

"Well, she only grabbed enough clothes to last her a few days, so she'll be back," Detective Nelson replied.

"You think so? I mean, even though she knows that we're looking for her?"

"Yeah, because she's no different from all the others. Right up until the end, they all thought they were one step ahead of us. The parking lot was full of police cars yet she came to her apartment anyway, and that says a lot about her."

"Alright, so what are we gonna do about catching her?"

"Well, we got two choices. We can hit the streets and may get lucky or we can stake out her apartment and wait for her to come back."

"Why do I have the feeling that we're gonna choose the latter?"

"Cause you know me, and you learn fast," Detective

Nelson replied with a smirk. "Oh, and another thing. There was another girl with her and I see no signs of a roommate so she doesn't live here."

"You think she might live in the apartments?"

"It's a possibility."

"Well, maybe we'll get lucky and catch em both."

"Yeah, and come to think about it, we may have hit the jackpot."

"How?"

"Think about it—Tamaya knew the robbers, right?"

"Yeah, well at least that's what it looks like on the surveillance tape."

"Okay, well what if the robbers are from around here, too?"

"It wouldn't be too farfetched. I mean, they could get together to make plans and nobody would know any better. Then, when it's all said and done, they could come back home like nothing happened."

"Well, if the women are in fact involved, I think they'll give up peacefully once we corner them."

"And the men?"

"That's something different altogether because they're carrying assault weapons. Let's do this. Let's go back to the station and get prepared for what could be a long wait. Then, if and when we encounter them, we'll deal with 'em accordingly."

"Sounds good to me," Officer Chamber said before heading for the door. After taking one last look around, Detective Nelson walked out before closing the door behind him.

***

"Hey, there go another one," Tamaya whispered.

"Alright, so that makes three in the last hour or one every twenty minutes.

"Damn, we gon have to go handle our business and get out of there."

"That's what we practicing for ain't it? Ain't no reason why we shouldn't be out of there in less than two minutes."

"That ain't gon be no problem, but you see the traffic?"

"What bout it?"

"It's bumper to bumper, that's what?"

"It's rush hour and everybody tryin to get home. We gon hit the bank in the morning so we should be good."

"I hope so cause ain't no way we gon be able to drive in this kind of traffic."

"Well, if anything happens, we can make it to the car on foot."

"On foot?"

"Yeah, either that or your ass is going to jail."

"That ain't an option," Tamaya replied while imagining herself running down 27th Avenue carrying a bag of money and an assault rifle.

"Well, you better keep up if it comes to that."

"Boy, I don't remember the last time I ran nowhere. Just my luck, I'll probably pass out."

"No, you won't, and even if you did, I'll pick you up and carry you."

"Stop lying!"

"Nah, real shit. I mean, you think I want to see you go to jail?"

"Probably the only reason you don't is because you want some more pussy."

"Oh, I'll admit, the pussy's good, but that ain't the only reason."

"Oh, no?"

"Nah, I actually like you. You're cute, finer than a ma'fucker, and you bout it. What more can a nigga ask for?"

"Yeah, well if I would've known that the dick was as good as it is, I probably would've giving you some a long time ago."

"Girl, you crazy."

"Shit, I'm for real and this getting money shit just makes it even better."

"Yeah, I hear you. Now, listen, be ready to handle your business day after tomorrow."

"Oh, you better believe I'll be ready, but what we gon do till then?"

"I'm sure we can find something to do," he said with a smirk.

"Yeah, I bet we can, too," she replied with a mischievous grin.

"Alright, well look. We saw what we needed to see so let's get out of here."

"Okay, but remember Snag said he wanted you to pick up something to smoke on the way back."

"Yeah, I remember," Curt shot back before heading for the door, and as Tamaya followed him out to the car, he climbed in, started it up, and headed back to the hotel.

***

"Mmm!" Crystal moaned while enjoying the pleasure Snag was giving her. Suddenly looking down at him, she couldn't help but smile to herself as he continued his oral onslaught. Twenty minutes earlier, he'd just stepped out of the shower when he heard somebody knocking on the door, and answering it naked, he was surprised when he saw Crystal on the other side. After jumping back in the shower, he'd given her a bath. While she sucked him off, he couldn't wait to return the favor.

Now, as he knelt between her legs listening to her moan with pleasure, he gently teased her clit while licking and sucking her pussy with abandon.

"You like that?" He suddenly asked while looking up at her.

"Mmm hmm!" she replied softly.

"Good, cause I got something else for you," he shot back while standing. Then, as he leaned forward to kiss her passionately, he grabbed his dick and began rubbing it up and down through the fields of her warm, wet pussy.

"Damn, you're wet," he said while positioning himself at her opening, and much to her delight, he entered her with one swift stroke.

After spreading her legs further, he began sliding his dick in and out of her with long deep strokes, and squeezing her pussy muscles tightly, Crystal closer her eyes and moaned with pleasure.

Settling into a rhythm, Snag buried himself inside of her

over and over again. And suddenly increasing his pace, he fucked her hard and fast while reaching up to gently massage her breast.

Biting her bottom lip, Crystal could feel her orgasm building as Snag continued pounding his dick in and out of her. Staring up at him lustfully, she felt a wave of pleasure wash over her as she came and coated his dick with her juices.

Suddenly pushing him back, she climbed down off the sink and motioned for him to take a seat on the toilet. Then, after he complied, she placed him at her opening before sitting down and taking him inside of her. Wrapping her arms around his neck, she began riding him slowly as he reached down to gently massage her ass.

Damn! Snag said to himself as she slid up and down on his dick and suddenly reaching up to pull her down onto him, he pushed up into her with every stroke. Determined to please him, Crystal squeezed her pussy muscles around him while continuing to ride him. Noticing his quickening pace, she knew it wouldn't be long.

Minutes later, she felt his body tense up and knew that he was on the verge of cumming. Catching him by surprise, she climbed off his lap, leaned down, and took him in her mouth.

"Mmm, shit!" he screamed as she began sucking him in and out of her mouth. Excited beyond his wildest dreams, he came flooding her mouth with his seed.

"Mmm!" Crystal moaned softly while swallowing every drop and gently massaging his balls. She was determined to get it all. As he looked on in amazement, she continued licking and sucking him in and out of her mouth. She looked up at him and smiled.

"You like that?"

"Hell, yeah! You gon fuck round and drive a nigga crazy."

"You think?"

"Shit, if you keep doing what you just did, I know."

"Yeah, well, if you think that's something, wait till you see what else I got in store for you."

"Oh, yeah?"

"Yeah," she said before walking out and with Snag right behind her, he couldn't wait to see just what she hand in mind.

CHAPTER 44

"Hey, Trigga, man you know them crackas just left from round here," his neighbor said as he slid he key into the lock."

"What crackas?"

"The damn police, who you think?"

"So, what they said?"

"I don't know cause I ain't come outside but they did knock on your door, and when nobody answered, they just left."

"So, if you ain't come outside, how you know they was the police?"

"Cause I was looking out my window."

"Alright, good lookin out," Trigga said before opening his door, and as his neighbor walked off, he stepped inside his apartment and closed the door behind him. He'd already had the feeling that they'd want to talk to him because of situation with Ray Ray, and now he wondered what's next. The car Ray Ray was in was registered to him, but was that the reason they came to his apartment, he asked himself while thinking about the incident with Chevy and the two niggas from the Silver Blue Apartments. Having no way of knowing, he knew that he had to do something.

"Damn!" he said to himself while contemplating his next move, and not knowing when they'd come back, he knew he had to get out of there before they did.

Rushing into his bedroom, he grabbed his AK-47 and two sixty round clips out of his closet before taking a seat on the bed. Then after removing several boxes of ammunition from the dresser drawer, he began filling the clips. Methodically inserting round after round, Trigga thought back to how his car had looked with Ray Ray inside, and the more he thought about it, the madder he became.

After finishing several minutes later, he grabbed a roll of duct tape from the kitchen and taped the two clips together. A hundred and twenty rounds were enough for him to handle his business, and if the police showed up, hey they'd get it, too. Now that he'd taken care of that, he grabbed a duffel bag from the closet and after making his way back over to the bed, he grabbed the mattress and flipped it over to reveal the two hundred and seventy five grand he'd stashed.

Grabbing the stacks of money, he placed them in a the bag before zipping it closed. Then grabbing the AK and both clips off the bed, he headed for the door. Suddenly thinking about the possibility of the police coming back, he pulled back the blinds and carefully scanned the parking lot. After being sure that the coast was clear, he opened the door and hurried over to the car and quickly climbing in, he threw the duffel bag in the backseat before starting the car, putting it in gear, and driving off to go handle his business.

***

"Alright, everybody listen up," Detective Nelson said to the officers he'd handpicked specifically for the surveillance team. "Now, I'm not gonna stand up here and preach to you about how to do your job because all of you have shown that you're more than capable of doing just that, but there are some things that I'd like to go over with you. After I'm finished, we can all begin preparing for our assignment. The first thing I want to address is the fact that this woman Tamaya Taylor may or may not be involved, but the men who are considered armed and extremely dangerous.

"They are suspects of at least two bank robberies, one in which two of our fellow officers were killed and I can't stress enough how important it is that we get 'em off the streets. In front of you is a folder containing your individual assignments, from where you'll be situated, to what you'll be doing. Stick to the plan because the last thing we need to do is to spook 'em. Officer Glasco!"

"Yes, sir."

"You will be positioned inside the apartment so I'll need you to stay alert. I've spoken with the manager of the complex so he'll be aware of our presence. If they're all from around there, they'll come back because it's familiar territory. It's where they feel the most comfortable and trust me, it's where we're most likely to catch them."

"Okay, I have a question," somebody suddenly blurted out.

"Alright, let's hear it."

"What are we supposed to do if we spot someone who looks suspicious or who we think could be involved?"

"Well, if that situation arises, we'll err on the side of caution. We'll detain 'em until we're sure they're not one of the people we're looking for. Keep in mind that Ms. Taylor is the primary target, but she could also be the link to the others so keep your eyes open."

"Are there any leads on possible suspects?"

"Well, we have a few that we're following up on but from what we've got so far, our suspects are African American, early to mid-twenties, and they're heavily organized. They also aren't afraid to shoot which is evident by the killings of our two fellow officers. If you encounter them, do not attempt to confront them on your own. Call for backup immediately. Then wait for them to arrive. They're carrying high powered assault weapons with high compacity magazines and they won't hesitate to shoot."

"So, what if we're spotted, and they make a run for it?"

"We pursue them, but be extremely cautious. Remember, these individuals have already killed two officers and they won't hesitate to kill more if they're backed into a corner. Any more questions? Alright then, I want everybody to start getting ready because we'll be departing in less than an hour. Once we get to the apartments, everybody will get in position, and then we'll wait to see what happens."

***

"Hey, ain't that Crystal's car?" Tamaya asked as Curt pulled in the hotel's parking lot.

"Where?"

"Right there," she replied pointing.

"Shit, I hope it is."

"Damn, why you gotta say it like that?"

"No reason, but if that is it, at least we ain't gotta keep that nigga company."

"Boy, you crazy. Come on," she said while climbing out of the car and following close behind her, all Curt could think about was getting her up to the room.

"I want to stop by to see if she's alright."

"Trust me, she is alright," Curt replied with a smirk. And after finally making it up the stairs, they approached the door and knocked several times. Receiving no response, Tamaya knocked again and seconds later the door swung open.

"Where my friend?" Tamaya asked.

"In the bathroom," Snag replied as she pushed past him, and turning to watch her walk towards the bathroom, Curt stepped into the room.

"Damn, y'all need to open a window or something."

"Man, look."

"Damn, nigga I'm just fucking with you," Curt said cutting him off. "Anyway, here," he said while handing him the bag of weed.

"What's this?"

"What you think it is?"

"Oh, yeah, I hope it's fire."

"Since when have you ever known me to smoke some bullshit?"

"Never."

"Alright then, it's fire," Curt said.

"Yeah, alright, so what y'all gettin ready to do?"

"Shit, the same thing y'all was doing before we got here."

"I feel you, but you know we still need to sit down and figure out what we gon do?"

"Yeah, I know, but right now I'm going next door to relieve some stress and get my head right."

"Damn man, you need to start taking this shit serious cause."

"Hey, you ready?" Tamaya suddenly asked interrupting them.

"Yeah, just give me a minute."

"Look, let me get the key and you can come when you're done."

"Alright, here." He said, and while reaching out to hand her the keys, Crystal came out of the bathroom and climbed under the covers.

"Man, look, I'll just holla back at you bout that," Curt said after noticing her and not wanting to talk in front of her, Snag reluctantly agreed.

"Yeah, whatever man," and after watching Curt and Tamaya walk out, he closed the door behind him before climbing back into bed with Crystal.

CHAPTER 45

"So, what you gotta holla at him bout?" Tamaya asked as she opened the door and stepped inside the room.

"You know bout what we gon do as far as leaving Miami."

"So, have you decided what you gon do?"

"Well, I got people in Georgia so if push comes to shove, that's where I'm going."

"What about me?"

"What you mean, what about you?"

"Just what I said."

"Shit, you can come with me to Georgia."

"Alright, so what Snag gon do?"

"I don't know. I mean, the nigga been acting kind of funny lately so I don't know what's on his mind."

"Why you ain't ask him?"

"Huh?"

"I said, why you ain't ask him what's on his mind. I mean, that's your friend, right?"

"Yeah, but at the same time, he's grown," Curt replied while rolling a joint.

"Well, that's on y'all. All I want to know is are we coming back here after we handle our business?"

"Probably, but I was thinking bout getting a room somewhere else. What you think?"

"It really don't make no difference to me. I mean, I was just asking cause I wanted to know what was up."

"Well, we'll see. At the same time, I'm gon get a car. Then, all we'll have to do is handle our business and get missing."

"I know that's right," Tamaya replied smiling.

"Hey, you want to hit this?" Curt suddenly asked.

"Hell, yeah! You think you the only one who want to get their head right?"

"Nah, but I ain't know if you wanted to hit it."

"Mmm hmm! Right," she said while taking the joint from him. After putting it to her lips, she inhaled deeply.

"Alright now, that's that fire," and no sooner had the words left his mouth before Tamaya began coughing uncontrollably.

"See, I told you."

"Damn, this shit's potent," she said as her eyes begin watering and after handing the joint back to Curt, she began undressing.

"Damn, what you doing?"

"I'm going to take a shower, why?"

"Just wondering."

"Well, I ain't had a shower since this morning and I'm feeling all sticky."

"Oh, I'll get you sticky alright."

"Damn, that's all you think about?"

"No, but man, let's go take a shower," he said in frustration and after taking a few steps in the direction of the bathroom, Tamaya stopped and turned.

"So, you coming or what?"

"Coming where?"

"To take shower with me?"

"Damn, didn't you just—"

"Boy, you know I was just playing," she said cutting him off.

"Girl, you need to make up your mind."

"Alright, come on," she said before walking off, and not having to be told twice, Curt quickly undressed and followed her into the bathroom.

Stepping into the shower, Tamaya turned on the water as Curt climbed in behind her and as the water began raining down on them, she grabbed the soap and rag and began lathering it up. Reaching around her, Curt grabbed the rag and began bathing her and suddenly becoming aroused, he reached one hand down between her legs.

Spreading her legs wider, Tamaya felt herself becoming wetter and suddenly without a word, Curt dipped his and entered her from behind. Positioning one leg up on the side of the tub and both hands firmly on the wall, she pushed back into him as he slammed into her over and over.

Gripping her hips tightly, he pulled her into him with every stroke and while fucking her with long deep strokes, he concentrated on satisfying her totally. Hearing her moan with pleasure, he knew that she was enjoying it as much as he was, and planting his feet firmly, he suddenly increased his pace.

Meanwhile, Tamaya couldn't believe that getting fucked in the shower could feel so good and as Curt continued pounding his dick in and out of her, she bit her bottom lip and pushed back into him.

Minutes later, she felt the tension building, and wanting him to cum with her, she reached back between her legs and began massaging his balls. Suddenly, the orgasm hit her from out of nowhere making her knees weak, and riding the wave of pleasure, she squeezed her pussy muscles around his dick.

It didn't take long for the tingling sensation to begin at the base of his spine and work its way up through his stomach and after burying himself deep inside of her, he came, flooding her insides.

Damn! he said to himself while releasing his seed and suddenly reaching around to caress her breasts, he smiled because he knew that this was only the beginning.

***

"Damn, nigga, come on," Blue said before walking out of the door of the McDonald's Restaurant.

"Man, what you rushing to get back over there for?" Craig replied after following him out.

"Cause we got shit to do, or you forgot?"

"Nah, I ain't forget, but how we gon do all that with them crackas round there?"

"That's the beauty of it cause they ain't worrying bout us," Blue said as they finally reached the car. "All they worried about is what happened earlier."

"Well, shit, we the cause of that."

"Yeah, but they don't know that. Besides, we live round there so we got an excuse for being over there."

"Alright, but let me ask you this. How we gon explain why the windows shot out the ma'fucking car?"

"We ain't gon have to cause we gon pull on 17th Avenue and walk through the gate by the Popeye's Chicken Restaurant."

"Hold up! I thought we was gon get a trap for that nigga Trigga."

"We are."

"So, how we supposed to be doing that if we gon leave the car by Popeye's?"

"We gon only leave it there til the police leave. By then, we should be ready to do what we gon do."

"Alright, but who gon be in the car?"

"What you mean?"

"You said that one of us was gon be posted up in the car by the front gate, right?"

"Yeah."

"And when the nigga Trigga drives up in the parking lot, we gon use the car to block the entrance."

"Right."

"So which one of us gon be in the car?"

"Do it matter? I mean, cause whoever's in the car once the entrance is blocked off, he gon get out so we can go ahead and handle our business."

"Alright, and then what we gon do?"

"What you think? We gon get missing before them crackas get there. After a few days, they'll be gone and we won't have to worry bout Trigga no more. Then, we can get back to getting money."

"Yeah, I hear you." Craig said as they drove past the apartments. After making a right on 17th Avenue, Blue pulled up in the parking lot and parked.

"You see anybody?"

"Nah, but that don't mean they ain't there."

"Yeah, I know, that's why we gon leave the car here," Blue said before climbing out of the car and as Craig climbed out after him, they looked around cautiously.

"So, what you think?"

"Bout what?"

"Bout what we doing. I mean, you think we can make it to the apartment?"

"Shit, we here now."

"Yeah, but whether or not them crackas gon fuck with us is another story."

"Well, ain't but one way to find out. Come on," Blue said before walking off. After stepping through the hole in the gate behind the Popeye's Chicken Restaurant, they headed for the apartment.

"Man, slow down." Craig suddenly said.

"Nah, nigga, you hurry up. What, you think we got all day to be out here bullshittin?"

"Nah."

"Well, come on," Blue said as they finally made it to the stairs. Just when they started up, they were caught off guard by two police officers who came down the stairs toward them.

Fuck! Craig said to himself as they suddenly made eye

contact. Trying hard to keep his nerves in check, he cut his eyes away from them as they passed. *Just keep going,* he said to himself while resisting the urge to look back. Finally making it to the top of the stairs, he noticed Blue right on his heels.

Approaching the apartment, he slid the key in the lock and unlocked the door. Then, after pushing it open, he stepped inside as Blue came in right behind him, and finally breathing a sigh of relief, he reached back and slammed the door shut.

Meanwhile, the men inside of the maintenance van downstairs had just recorded their every move.

CHAPTER 46

"Hey, did you guys get that?" Detective Nelson asked after watching Craig and Blue walk into the apartment.

"Yeah, we got 'em," one of the men inside the surveillance van replied.

"Okay, now run their pictures through the facial recognition program and let's see what comes back on them."

"I'm already on it, so just relax, detective," came the reply and while sitting in his unmarked car with Officer Chambers at the far end of the parking lot, he felt himself becoming anxious.

"Is this your first stakeout?" He asked trying to make conversation.

"Yeah, you can say that," Officer Chambers replied.

"Well, it can get pretty boring at times and there's no guarantees that anything will come of it."

"There are no guarantees in life, detective, but if this is what it takes to catch the son of a bitch who robbed the bank and killed our fellow officers, there's no place I'd rather be."

"Now, that's what I like to hear."

"Alright, we got a hit," a voice suddenly said on the radio.

"What you got?"

"Well, out of them is Craig Larkin, age twenty five and all of this arrests have been for drug related crimes. The most recent being two months ago."

"Okay, what about the other one?"

"He's Justin Harris, age twenty seven, and he's served seven years for aggravated assault with a deadly weapon. He was released three months ago."

"Alright, let me know if you come with anything else."

"Will do, sir."

"Sergeant Glasco, you there?"

"Yes, sir."

"Is everything alright? I mean, do you need some help in there?"

"Nah, I'm good, but I found her diary and I think you'd find some of the things in it quite interesting."

"Yeah, I'm sure I will but is there anything in it that'll help us with the investigation?"

"I'm still reading so that's yet to be determined."

"Okay, well, keep at it. We need something, anything that'll tell us whether or not she's involved."

"I'm on it."

"Good, and Glasco..."

"Yes, sir."

"You might as well get comfortable because we might be in for a long wait."

"I've been there before so this is nothing new."

"Yeah, well, if you need anything just call."

"Will do, sir."

"Good, over. Now, what do you know about this area?"

"Other than the fact that most of the residents are on section 8 and that the complex is plagued by drug sales and violence, not much."

"Sounds like you know plenty." Detective Nelson replied with a smirk. "And believe it or not, you're right on all accounts."

"Yeah, but the thing that gets me is how can so many people be struggling and not do anything to improve their conditions? The young men here would rather rob and sell drugs instead of getting a job, and the girls feel like the more babies they have, the bigger the welfare check."

"You know, people have been trying to understand that for years because not only are more young men in jail or prison than in college, but more kids are being born into poverty than ever before."

"So, what do you think can be done to stop the trend?"

"Well, the first thing we need to do is get rid of the bad elements. One bad apple will spoil the whole box, right?"

"Yeah."

"And one bad individual can spoil half a neighborhood or more. So, you get rid of those few and you just may have a chance."

"So, in other words we're on the front lines?"

"Exactly, and I know at times it may seem like we're losing the battle, but that's alright."

"What!"

"I said it's alright if we lose a few battles."

"And what makes you say that?"

"Because the goal is to win the war. Now, let's keep our eyes open for Ms. Taylor," Detective Nelson said suddenly changing the subject.

"Yeah, alright," Officer Chambers replied, and while still thinking about the conversation, he wondered to himself if they were in fact fighting a war that could be won at all.

****

"Damn, girl, you better slow down. You remember what happened the last time you hit that shit like you was crazy," Curt said while lying in bed with Tamaya smoking a joint.

"Look, I got this, you just concentrate on getting this back up," she replied before reaching down the grab him limp dick.

"Damn, what you go do, fuck me to death?"

"Nah, but I'm gon put this pussy on you so you ain't got no reason to be looking at another bitch."

"Say what!"

"You heard what I said."

"Yeah, but why you worryin about that? I mean, a nigga got way more important shit to be worryin bout."

"Mmm hmm! I hear you but I know how y'all niggas is. A bitch could give you all the pussy and head y'all can handle and y'all gon still try to find another bitch to fuck."

"Hold up! How you just gon put me in that category?"

"Cause you a nigga, that's why."

"But damn, we just started kickin it. Plus, after all, the other shit we like Bonnie and Clyde up in this ma'fucker,"

Curt said laughing.

"Oh, so you got jokes, huh? All the police in Miami looking for us and you joking. Boy, that shit ain't funny."

"So, why are you laughing?"

"Cause of this," he said while pointing, and suddenly looking down, she notice his dick standing at attention.

"Boy!"

"Well, you the one who said that you was waitin for it to get back hard."

"Yeah, but—"

"Oh, so what you gon leave a nigga hanging like this?" He asked cutting her off.

"No, because I did tell you that, but when we finish, we need to talk."

"Bout what?"

"You know, this whole situation, us, the bank, and what we gon do about Snag, and if we decide to go anywhere, where we going cause you know like I know that the longer we stay here, the more likely them crackas gon eventually find us."

"Yeah, but after we get this money, shit gon be different."

"How?"

"Cause we'll have enough money to go somewhere far away from here, then we won't have to worry bout nothing."

"I hope so," Tamaya said as she began massaging him up and down trying to imagine what would happen if they were confronted by the police. Then, she climbed up and straddled him. After reaching back between her legs, she grabbed him before placing him at her opening. As he reached around to grab her ass firmly, she lowered herself down onto him.

Tamaya couldn't imagine herself doing time as she began riding him and suddenly coming to grips with the only other option, she made up her that getting caught wasn't an option.

***

"What's wrong?"

"Nothing, I mean, everything," Snag replied while lying in bed with Crystal. "I'm just thinking bout how fucked up this situation we done got ourselves in is."

"What, the bank robberies?"

"Yeah, and then you get the two police who got killed."

"Well, let me ask you something. What made y'all decide to rob a bank in the first place?"

"Paper chasin."

"Huh?"

"Tryin to get some money. I mean, that's what it's all about, ain't it? Everything we do in life about getting a dollar. Whether you rob, get a job, hustle, steal, or whatever. It all boils down to the same thing, everybody's chasin paper."

"Yeah, but now look what done happened."

"What's done is done, and ain't nothing we can say or do that's gon change it. Then, you got him walking round acting like everything's alright."

"Have you tried talkin to him bout it?"

"Yeah, but it ain't do no good cause his whole attitude is like fuck them crackas."

"Okay, but that's him you gotta look out for you."

"Yeah, but I can't just leave him."

"Why not? I mean, he grown and he can take care of himself, can't he?"

"Yeah. But we started this shit together."

"Oh, so, that means y'all gotta die together?"

"Look, ain't nobody dyin."

"Yeah, I'll bet that's what y'all said before those two police got killed."

"Now that wasn't supposed to happen."

"Mmm hmm! I hear you," Crystal said sarcastically.

"Nah, I'm serious. That's the main reason we set the two minute timeline, so by the time the police got there, we'd be gone."

"So, what happened?"

"I don't know, but when we came out of the bank, they was right there. I think they spotted the car and decided to run the tag for some reason."

"Yeah, well, right now the police are looking everywhere for y'all and something gon have to give cause they ain't gon stop."

"No, but the good thing is that they don't know about you. I don't know what I'd do if I got you in trouble."

"Well, I don't know what I can do to help, but if you need me to do anything, just let me know."

"Yeah, alright." Snag replied before kissing her passionately.

"Damn, why I couldn't have met you months ago?"

"I've asked myself that a hundred times," she said smiling.

"Yeah, well don't worry. I'll figure something out."

"I hope so," she said to herself as he climbed between her

legs. After positioning himself at her opening, he buried himself inside of her as a lone tear fell from her eye.

CHAPTER 47

"Alright, so now what we just gon sit up in this ma'fucker doing nothing?" Craig asked while sitting in the living room with Blue.

"Nah, we gon chill til them crackas leave unless you just want to walk downstairs with the choppa while they out there."

"Nah, I'm good but I'm just sayin..."

"Sayin what?"

"That I'm ready to handle our business so we can get back to doing what we do."

"I'm feelin that, but at the same time. patience is a virtue. Besides, if that nigga rides through here, it ain't like he knows where we stay."

"True, but I'm just ready to get it over with."

"Trust me, it's gon come. All we gotta do is be ready when it do."

"Believe me, you ain't gotta worry bout that."

"Hey, when's the last time you saw Tamaya and her

friend?"

"Shit, I don't know, but what made you ask bout them?"

"Just wondering that's all."

"Yeah, well, I ain't seen em since all this shit started with Trigga. Matter of fact, the last time I saw 'em, they was leaving with them two niggas from downstairs."

"Oh, yeah, them niggas Curt and what's the other nigga's name?"

"Snag."

"Yeah, that's right. But I mean, what's up, you ain't fucking with her no more?"

"It ain't that, it's just—oh, shit!"

"What's wrong?"

"Man, look, that's Tamaya's picture on the damn TV."

"What the—"

"Damn, turn it up," Craig said cutting him off and after turning up the volume, they both stared at the screen as the reporter spoke.

> "We interrupt the regular scheduled program to bring you new developments in a pending investigation. The police have identified a person of interest in the bank robbery that resulted in the deaths of two police officer earlier this week, and they're urging anyone with information regarding the whereabouts of the woman pictured on the screen to call the police. Tamaya Taylor has been identified as a person of interest, and while she is not being called a suspect, the police would like to question her. Again, if anyone knows her

> whereabouts, you are being urged to call the police. If you wish to remain anonymous, call the number at the bottom of your screen. Now, back to your regularly scheduled program."

"Damn, you heard what that ma'fucker said," Craig asked in disbelief.

"Hell, yeah, and we round here trying to figure out who was robbing them banks. Shit, she down with 'em."

"Wait a minute! You don't think it's them downstairs?"

"Who, them niggas Curt and Snag?"

"Yeah."

"Hell, nah!"

"Why not?"

"Cause them niggas ain't on nothing, that's why. I mean, they still ridin round in that raggedy ass blue car."

"Yeah, but I don't know. They was driving a ma'fuckin Escalade the last time I saw 'em, and come to think about it, we ain't seen them niggas in a lil minute either."

"Well, I'll be damn. All the while we been tryin to figure out who was robbing them banks, and them ma'fuckas been downstairs the whole time."

"That's probably why Tamaya's fuckin with him. You know, she ain't fuckin with a nigga if he ain't got no money."

"Yeah, well, the reporter said that two police got killed so if it was them, they done fucked up."

"That's on them. I'm tryin to think where they could've stashed the money."

"Why, you gon try to rob 'em?"

"Why not? Ain't no need to let them crackas get it back,

you feel me?"

"Yeah, but damn, I still can't believe them square ass niggas robbing banks."

"Look, we was just sleepin on them niggas and just because they ain't bout what we bout, it don't mean they square. Shit, if that's the case, we square cause they robbing banks and we ain't."

"Whatever, man, so now I guess after we handle our business with Trigga, we gon see bout robbing them for the money they robbed for?"

"Ain't no see bout in it, that's what we gon do," Blue replied.

"Alright, but I hope you know that we might have to murk 'em too cause I just don't see 'em coming up off that money so easy, especially after going through what they went through to get it."

"It didn't make no difference to me cause if we don't do it, the police definitely will. I'm just trying to get the money from 'em before the police get it cause trust me, when them crackas find out it's them they comin."

"Yeah, I hear you," Craig said and suddenly thinking about how far things had gone. Lately, he had started wondering whether it was all worth it.

***

"Alright, people. Look alive, we've got company." Detective Nelson said into his radio as he looked up to see a car driving into the complex.

"We're on it," A voice replied.

"Okay, the car's a black Nissan Altima with a lone male driver. He's wearing a hat so I couldn't get a good look at him. But the tag number Alpha, Lima, Kilo, three, zero, five, you copy?"

"Loud and clear, but we can't get a clear visual on him either."

"Shit!"

"What do you want us to do?"

"Sit tight. Let's see what he does." Detective Nelson replied while contemplating his next move.

"Okay, the car's registered to a Brittany Morris," the voice suddenly said over the radio.

"Alright, but that's definitely not her driving."

"Well, if you want, we could try."

"No, everyone keep your positions," Detective Nelson said cutting him off.

"So what, we just gon do nothing?" Officer Chambers suddenly asked.

"Look, if we move prematurely, we could jeopardize the whole thing and we may not get another chance like this."

"Okay, but suppose whoever driving the car is involved?"

"If he is, he's just scoping out the area and as long as he doesn't detect anything unusual, he'll come back."

"And you know this how?"

"Human nature. You see, if he is somehow involved in all of this, what is he riding around here looking for? And why even ride through here at all? I mean, I can understand you wanting to catch these guys but remember there was two of them and there's only one person in that car."

"So what, you just gon let him go?"

"For now, yes, because as long as he thinks the coast is clear, he'll be back."

"Hey, he's headed back your way, detective," the voice suddenly said over the radio.

"Yeah, we have him in sight," Detective Nelson replied as the car headed in their direction.

"What you do want us to do?"

"Hold tight, I'm thinking."

"Yeah, and he's approaching the exit."

"You think I don't know that."

"Detective, he's getting away. What do you want us to do?"

"Stand down for now."

"We could have a car stop him down the street."

"No, let him go. As long as he thinks it's clear, he'll be back."

"And what if he decides not to come back?"

"Then, I'll take the blame," Detective Nelson replied, and while sitting there contemplating his decision, he hoped that he'd done the right thing.

Meanwhile, after driving out of the parking lot, Trigga was already formulating a plan in his head. He'd seen what he needed to see, and when they least expected it, he'd be back.

CHAPTER 48

"I'm hungry," Tamaya said before sitting up in bed.

"Yeah, me too," Curt replied. "I tell you what, let's take a quick shower and then we'll go get us some breakfast."

"Alright," Tamaya said while climbing out of bed, and as she headed for the bathroom, he climbed out of bed while thinking about what he had to do today. First, they'd stop somewhere to get them something to eat. Then, they'd start getting ready for tomorrow. Last night, while laying in bed, he'd decided to steal two cars and place them at both of the prearranged locations. That way, if anything happens, they would have the option of going to either spot, and no matter what, there would be a car waiting for them.

"Alright, I'm done," Tamaya suddenly said while coming out of the bathroom.

"Yeah, alright, just give me a minute."

"I don't know why you ain't just take shower with me."

"Cause you know damn well we'd still be in there, that's why," he replied smiling.

"Yeah, well, hurry up cause my stomach's growling."

"Yeah, yeah alright," Curt said before disappearing in the bathroom, and as she began dressing, all Tamaya could think about was how fast her life had went from sugar to shit. She had to admit that the dick was good and a lil drama ain't hurt nobody, but having all the police in Miami looking for you was a bit much by any standard.

Suddenly, Curt came out of the bathroom and began getting dressed, and deciding to go next door, Tamaya headed for the door.

"Where you going?" He asked.

"Next door to see if Crystal and Snag want us to bring them back something to eat."

"Alright, but you know we ain't coming right back."

"So, how long you think we gon be gone?"

"Shit, I don't know. I mean, first we gon stop to get something to eat. Then, we gotta find two cars."

"Two!"

"Yeah, I decided to leave one in each spot. That way, if anything happens and we can't get to one, we'll have the other one."

"Oh, alright, but what could happen?"

"Trust me, a whole lot," Curt replied while thinking back to when they'd come out of the bank to find the police waiting for them in the parking lot.

"Yeah, well, if we go in, handle our business, and get out of there, we should be alright."

"True, but you still gotta be prepared just in case."

"Alright, but right now, you need to hurry up cause I'm hungry," Tamaya said before walking out. Suddenly stopping in front of the room next door, she knocked. Seconds later, the door opened.

"Where's Curt?" Snag asked.

"He's coming, where's Crystal?"

"In the bathroom."

"Well, we goin to get something to eat so I came over to see if y'all wanted us to bring all something back?"

"Where y'all going?"

"It depends on what y'all want?"

"Well, just—"

"Hey girl!" Crystal suddenly screamed cutting him off.

"What's up?"

"Just came over to see if y'all wanted something to eat?"

"Hell, yeah, I'm starving."

"Alright, what y'all want?"

"Just bring me whatever you get."

"Alright, what about you?" she asked facing Snag.

"Shit, I don't know, just bring me something."

"Okay, I'll tell Curt."

"Tell me what?" Curt suddenly asked after getting through the door.

"Snag said just bring him something."

"Alright, what about Crystal?"

"I'll get her something," Tamaya replied.

"Yeah, alright."

"So what's up, nigga, you good?" Curt asked while eyeing his friend.

"Yeah, but we still need to talk."

"Yeah, yeah I hear you. Anyway, let's get out of here so we can get back."

"Yeah, and y'all be careful cause them crackas had Tamaya's picture on the TV last night."

"What!"

"Last night, they had her picture on the TV talking bout how all they want to do is talk to her."

"Man, that's bullshit."

"I know, that's why I'm tellin y'all to be careful."

"Alright, we got you." Curt replied before walking off, and after finally making it downstairs to the car, they both climbed in before Curt started it up and drove out the parking lot.

***

"Man, I still can't believe them niggas robbing banks," Blue said as he spotted his friend coming down the hallway.

"Shit, I can't believe Tamaya's down with 'em," Curt replied.

"Why not? I mean, she's just like the rest of them gold digging ho's."

"Probably, but robbing a bank... Man, that's some G shit. You got niggas who won't try no shit like that."

"Yeah, I know, but they fucked up when they killed those two police."

"Yeah, cause them crackas ain't gon never stop looking for they ass."

"That's why we gotta figure out where they got the money stashed."

"Man, look. First, you talkin bout settin a trap for Trigga. Now, you talkin bout robbing the niggas downstairs. How the fuck we supposed to do all that and still keep the spot running?"

"Man, fuck that spot for right now. Them niggas done hit banks so I know they got over a hundred stacks."

"Alright, but what about Trigga?"

"We go ahead and deal with him first. Then, while the police doing what they do, we'll run down on their ass."

"I'm with you, but man, we gotta be on point cause that nigga Trigga ain't bullshittin. We done murked two of his friends so you already know what time it is."

"Fuck that nigga, and when we run down on his ass, he gon get what his friends got."

"Alright, so when we supposed to do this shit with Trigga?"

"When it gets dark cause I doubt he gon come round here during the day."

"Why not?"

"Cause if I was trying to get at a nigga, that's what I'd do. Besides, during the day, ain't that much traffic comin up here. Now at night, you got all kinds of ma'fuckers coming and going so a nigga could blend in."

"Yeah, but he got us fucked up."

"Damn right, and by the time he figures it out, it's gon be too late."

"Alright, but let me ask you this. How we gon get the choppa out the car without everybody being all up in our business?"

"Shit, you remember what we did when we was going though it with them niggas from behind the P in Opa-Locka?"

"Yea, we dropped 'em out the window by the Lake and walked to the car that way."

"That's right, and don't forget that the car's still parked on 17th so it ain't nothing to walk to it without a ma'fucker being all up in your business."

"Alright, I'm feeling that," Craig said smiling.

"Nigga, I ain't new to this, I'm true to this," Blue replied. "And you of all people should know that by now."

"Yeah, but I mean, fuck it. I'm just ready to get it over with, you feel me?"

"Yeah, I feel you," Blue replied and suddenly thinking bout Curt and Snag, he wondered how they were going to get the money from them before the police did.

****

"Hey, Glasco!"

"Yes, sir."

"How you doin in there?" Detective Nelson asked.

"I'm good, detective. I got a 50 inch flat screen TV to look at, a queen size bed to lay in, and air conditioning. What more can a girl ask for?"

"You make work sound like a vacation."

"Well, when you get an assignment like mine, it almost feels like it."

"Yeah, well don't get too comfortable because Ms. Taylor could come through the door at any time."

"Trust me, detective. If she comes through that door, I'm going to ruin her day big time."

"Now, that's more like it. Anyway, I was calling to let

you know that I'm having some food delivered to you. He'll be dressed like a pizza man, but he's one of ours."

"Well, tell him he's definitely welcome cause I am hungry."

"Yeah, we all are. You just stay alert," Detective Nelson said and after speaking briefly to the men inside the surveillance van, he along with Officer Chambers continued waiting.

CHAPTER 49

Scanning the area carefully, Tamaya watched as Curt casually walked up the street to Miami shores in search of another car to steal. They'd just returned from dropping off the Dodge Charger he'd stolen earlier and although she'd witnessed it with her own eyes, she still couldn't believe how easy he made it look. Now, crouched low behind the steering wheel of Curt's car, she watched as he passed a house with a 2012 Chevy Camaro parked in the yard. In a blink of an eye, he doubled back before approaching it from the driver's side. Seconds later, he backed out of the driveway and right on cue, she followed as he turned the corner.

Following him out to north Miami Avenue, they made a right before driving down to 96th Street and after making a left, they headed west to 27th Avenue. Then, making another left, they drove south, and minutes later, they were pulling up in Clown City located on 64th Street. Finding an empty spot at the far end of the lot, he parked, got out, and jumped in the car with Tamaya.

"Alright, that's a wrap."

“You don’t think nobody gon bother ‘em?”

“Somebody might, that’s why we gon come by to check before we head over to the bank.”

“Alright, now what?”

“We go get us something to eat.”

“From where?”

“You know where Esters at?”

“Yeah.”

“Well, that’s where we’re headed,” Curt said as Tamaya pulled out into traffic. After reaching 46th Street, she made a left.

“What’s your job once we’re inside the bank?” Curt suddenly asked.”

“I’m supposed to watch everybody and make sure they don’t try nothing.”

“Okay, and if I go left, which way do you go?”

“Right.”

“Is there any particular place you need to be standing?”

“Not really, but it’s best to stand by the door just in case somebody comes in.”

“That’s right,” Curt said smiling, “Damn, most niggas don’t pick up on shit that fast.”

“Yeah, well, I just hope I ain’t gotta shoot nobody.”

“If we go in handle our business like we’re supposed to, it won’t come to that,” Curt replied as they pulled up to the light on 46th Street and 7th Avenue. Making a quick right, she slowed down the car before pulling up in front of Esters Restaurant.

“You coming?” Curt asked while climbing out of the car.

“Yeah,” Tamaya replied before climbing out after him,

and slamming the door behind them, they headed inside.

"Welcome to Esters, how many I help you?" the lady asked as they walked up to the counter.

"Yeah, give me two beef stew dinners," Curt replied.

"What would you like, white or yellow rice with that?"

"Yellow."

"You want greens or candy yams with that?"

"Yeah, both and some muffins."

"Alright, anything else?"

"Yeah, I would like two of the fried chicken dinners please." Tamaya said.

"Would you like baked beans and potato salad with that?"

"Yes, ma'am."

"Anything to drink?"

"Nah, but can we have two slices of chocolate cake and two of the red velvet?"

"Of course, just give me a minute," the lady said before walking off.

"So you ready?" Curt asked while turning to face her.

"For what?"

"For what?"

"For tomorrow."

"Oh, yeah," Tamaya replied.

"I hope so."

"Look, I ain't tryin to go to jail."

"I know, that's right," Curt said smiling. "Just think, by this time tomorrow, we'll be somewhere counting our money."

"Yeah, but then, we gon have to sit down and figure out what we gon next."

"Okay, here's your order, and that'll be thirty four dollars," the lady said while placing their food on the counter.

"Alright, here you go," Curt replied while handing her the money, and after grabbing their plates, they both walked back to the car. Then, after climbing in and starting it up, Curt put the car in gear and headed back to the hotel.

****

"Let me hit that."

"Nigga, roll your own," Blue replied.

"I don't feel like rolling one."

"Well, you don't want to smoke," Blue shot back while taking a hit of the joint.

"Damn nigga, you ain't gon let me hit that for real?"

"Man, here," Blue said in frustration.

"What time is it?"

"One o'clock, why?"

"Cause it seems like times moving slower than a ma'fucker."

"I thought I was the only one who felt like that."

"Nah, and it don't get dark til round seven thirty, eight."

"Yeah, I know, so what we gon do till then? I mean, cause I'm getting tired of sitting up in this ma'fucker doin nothing."

"Well, how bout we call some ho's over?"

"Who?"

"Shit, it don't matter cause by eight, they gon be gone anyway."

"Alright, fuck it, cause anything's better than this."

"I know that's right," Blue said while pulling out his phone, and as he flipped it open and began dialing a number, Craig took a long pull on the joint.

"Hello! Yeah, this Sherry? Hey, this Blue, what's up? Ain't nothing, just called to holla at you to see what you was up to? Yeah, well, I ain't doin nothing either so how bout you come by? Shit, that's cool cause I got somebody here she can talk to. You remember where I stay right? Yeah, in the Silver Blue Lakes Apartments. Alright, well I'll be here. Yeah, alright, bye," he said before hanging up.

"So what's up?" Craig asked as soon as he hung up.

"You remember Sherry?"

"From over by Olinda Park?"

"Yeah, that's her, she's coming by and she's bringing a friend with her."

"Man, I hope she ain't ugly."

"Look, they gon only be here til it's time for us to go handle our business."

"Alright, but what that gotta do with her being ugly?"

"Nothin, I'm just sayin don't be with that lovey dovey shit."

"Damn nigga, you act like I got a tender dick or something."

"I ain't saying that. All I'm saying is that it don't matter whether she's ugly or not."

"Nigga, you just sayin that cause she ain't comin over here for you."

"Damn, why you trippin it ain't like you gon marry her. We tryin to kill time til it gets dark and you worryin bout if the girl's ugly."

"Okay, and what's wrong with that?"

"Nothing, but don't act like you ain't never fucked with no ugly bitch."

"I ain't saying that."

"So, what are you sayin?"

"Nothin man, just fuck it. Matter of fact, where the damn weed at?"

"On the counter, why?"

"Cause I want to roll a joint that's why. That's alright with you?"

"Yeah, but a minute ago, you ain't feel like rolling none."

"Well, I do now. At least if she is ugly, I can say I ain't know."

"Nigga, you stupid," Blue said laughing. "Anyway, they'll be here soon so let's get ready. At the same time, don't forget what we gotta take care of later."

"Trust me, I ain't gone forget," Craig replied as he fired up the joint, and thinking about the situation with Trigga, Blue couldn't wait to put in work.

***

"Damn, where the fuck they went to Broward to get something to eat?" Snag screamed while pacing back and forth.

"Look, just calm down, they'll be back in a minute," Crystal replied.

"Calm down! I got all the police in Miami looking for me, I ain't got nowhere to go and you talkin about calm down.

Then if that ain't bad enough, you got Curt acting like his shit don't stank," and no sooner had the words left his mouth before they heard somebody knocking on the door. "That's probably them right there," he said while going to open it. Snatching it open, he came face to face with Curt and Tamaya.

"Damn, y'all could've cooked that shit faster than that."

"Yeah, whatever," Curt replied before brushing past him and after Tamaya followed him in, Snag slammed the door shut.

"Man, where y'all been?"

"Minding ours, now I got you something to eat so be thankful for that."

"Hold up! What you mean minding y'alls?"

"Just what I said."

"Well, in case you forgot, the police are still looking for Tamaya. They had her picture all over the damn TV and it's only a matter of time before they coming looking for us."

"Alright, and by then, we'll be long gone," Curt replied.

"You keep sayin that, but we ain't sat down and talking about nothing."

"What's to talk about?"

"Where we going, when we going, and how we gon get there."

"Look, you're grown and if you want to go, then go. I can take care of myself, and last time I checked, I ain't need no babysitter."

"I ain't say you did. All I'm saying is I thought we was gon ride this out together."

"Well, you thought wrong," Curt replied with a matter of

fact tone. “You do you and let me do me, alright?”

“Yeah, whatever man. You know what, I’m out of here,” Curt said as he headed for the door and rendered speechless, Tamaya and Crystal sat quietly as he walked out.

“Girl, I’ll come back and holla at you. Let me go over here and see what’s up.”

“Alright,” Crystal replied before watching her friend walk out the room, and still trying to make sense of what just happened, she looked over at Snag and had no idea what to say to him.

CHAPTER 50

"So, how you holding up?" Detective Nelson asked while cutting his eyes at Officer Chambers.

"Well, besides cramping, having to piss in a milk jug, and being bored, I'm having the time of my life."

"Well, you're planning to become a detective, so you'd better get used to it."

"It wouldn't be so bad if I didn't have to be cramped up in this car."

"What would you rather, do dress up like a bum and lay in a pissy gutter or sit up in this cramped car with me?"

"Well, you do have a point," Officer Chambers replied. "Hey, we got company," he said after suddenly spotting a car coming through the gate.

"Yeah, I see it," Detective Nelson replied as he looked up to see the car backing into a parking spot. "Alright, people, get ready."

"We're on him," a voice said over the radio and seconds later, when the driver still hadn't gotten out, everyone became suspicious.

"He's not getting out, people."

"You think he could be one of them?" Officer Chambers asked.

"It's a possibility. It could also be somebody waiting for someone."

"Yeah, well whoever it is he needs to show his face."

"Can you get a visual?"

"Negative, his shoulders are blocking his face."

"Shit! What's with everybody being so damn secretive?"

"Who knows what be on people's minds nowadays."

"You want me to send somebody?"

"No, stay in your position," Detective Nelson said cutting him off, and while contemplating their next move, he spotted another car pulling into the parking lot. "Heads up, people. We got another car pulling into the lot."

"We see it," one of the men inside the surveillance van replied.

"Wait a minute! It's the guy from earlier with the baseball hat. The one we couldn't get a visual on."

"Yeah, but he's driving a different car."

"So, what's he doing?"

"Nothing that I can see, wait! The first car's moving and it looks like he's leaving. Something's not right," Officer Chambers said, and while they looked on, Blue stopped the car blocking the entrance before jumping out with his AK and heading down the hall.

"Oh, shit! Did you just see that?"

"Yeah, it's an ambush. He's going to ambush the guy wearing the baseball cap!" Detective Nelson screamed, and as soon as the stepped out of his car the sound of automatic gunfire filled the air. “Shit! Somebody call for backup,” he said while drawing his gun!

“What’s going on!” Sergeant Glasco screamed over the radio.

“You just stay put. We can handle this,” Detective Nelson replied before taking off running. After quickly making his way down the hall, he spotted two men firing automatic weapons at the car that had just passed them.

Startled by the sound of footsteps behind him, he looked up to see Officer Chambers running toward him followed by three of the men from surveillance van.

“What the fuck are y’all doing?”

“Helping you, that’s what.”

“Well, our cover’s blown now so spread out,” Detective Nelson said, and as the men fanned out across the parking lot, he flipped the safety off of his gun and stood up.

“City of Miami police!” He screamed. Before he could say another word, the gunman turned and began firing in his direction.

“Fuck!” He screamed before ducking, and as broken glass began raining down on him, he contemplated what to do next.

Suddenly, the other officers began firing at the gunmen, and in spite of being outgunned, their marksmanship proved to be the deciding factor.

Mortally wounded, Blue looked down at Craig’s lifeless body laying behind the car and wondered to himself how the police got there so fast. Knowing that he had no other way out, he changed the clip in his AK-47 while coming to grips with the inevitable. Then, suddenly screaming at the top of his lungs, he came out firing before being cut down in a hail of bullets. As his body crumpled to the ground, Detective Nelson began trying to make sense of it all.

***

"Look, I said I don't want to talk about it," Curt said while walking away from Tamaya.

"Well, you need to," she replied before going after him.

"Man, fuck that nigga. Them crackas don't know shit bout us so what he panicking for?"

"Cause he don't want to go to jail."

"Well, he should've thought about that before he ran up in them crackas shit."

"Curt, that's your friend," Tamaya said almost pleadingly.

"And what's that supposed to mean?"

"That y'all don't need to be fallin out bout no stupid shit."

"Look, if push comes to shove and I have to leave, I ain't got no problem with that, but if I don't, I ain't going nowhere. He thinks that if we leave, we gon be alright, but what he don't understand is that if them crackas ever figure out who we is, ain't nothing gon stop them from looking for us. Two police got killed, you think them crackas as gon just forget about us?"

"No."

"So, it really don't make no difference if we leave or stay."

"Alright, so what's gon happen after we hit the bank?"

"It depends."

"On what?"

"On how shit goes. I mean, if everything goes like we planned, then we can come back and chill while we count our money."

"And if things don't go like we planned?"

"Then we might have to get missing," Curt replied "You gon have to lay low regardless cause they don had your face all over the damn TV."

"Yeah, I know, and I ain't trying to be fucked up with the crackas," Tamaya replied. "So, you ain't go talk to Snag?"

"For what? I'm gone tell you like I told him. If he wants to leave, that's him. I'm gon get this money and live like I want to live. Now, if you ain't feelin me, I'll respect it, but I'm going up in them crackas' shit tomorrow and it's whatever after that."

"Shit, I don't know what you talkin bout. I'm going with you. I just don't want to see you fall out with your friend."

"He'll be alright. Let's just get ready for tomorrow."

"Yeah, alright," Tamaya replied and suddenly smiling to herself, she couldn't wait for tomorrow morning.

***

Back at the Silver Blue Lakes Apartments, Detective Nelson reviewed what had just happened down to the smallest detail. But the thing that was bothering him was that he didn't know why it happened.

"Could somebody, anybody tell me something?"

"Well, the dead guy in the car has been identified as Lance Mitchell, age twenty five and get this. He's listed as a suspect in a homicide that happened in Opa-Locka a few days ago."

"Wait a minute! What was the victim's name?"

"Christopher Hawthorne."

"Son of a bitch!"

"What?"

"Hawthorne is the guy I told you about. You know, the one I sent to prison for robbing drug dealers. Only for him to get out and start selling drugs himself."

"Well, you know they found over two hundred thousand in the dead guy's car."

"Okay, so let's just say he robbed Hawthorne for the money. Why did the other two guys want him dead?"

"Maybe they wanted the money for themselves."

"Alright, but now the question is, how did they know he had it?"

"I don't know, maybe they led him to believe that they were gonna sell him something, but changed their minds and decided to kill him."

"No, I think it's something else."

"Wait a minute! Didn't they just have a shooting around here?"

"Yeah, why?"

"Because I'll bet you that these were the parties involved."

"Well, they did find an AK-47 in the dead guy's car, and I'll bet you that it's the gun used in the previous shooting."

"I tell you what, send a couple of the shell casings over to ballistics to see if we can get a match."

"Alright, and I'll tell 'em to put a rush on it."

"Okay, now what we got on the other two?"

"Not much, but we've got people searching the apartment."

"Alright, let me know the minute you find anything."

"Yes, sir," Officer Chambers replied before walking off, and after watching him go, all Detective Nelson could think about was what would happen next.

CHAPTER 51

"Hey, ain't that the apartments? Crystal asked while pointing at the TV."

"Yeah, but damn, I wonder what happened. Turn it up," he said, and after Crystal turned it up, he sat up in bed and listened carefully.

> "We're live in Northwest Miami Dade County on the scene of a deadly shooting where police say that three people lost their loves due to gun violence. From what we've learned so far, two assailants opened fire on a car occupied by Lance Mitchell, killing him instantly. After being confronted by the police, a shootout ensued resulting in the deaths of both gunmen. This is believed to be an ongoing feud that escalated into today's deadly shooting. The other two deceased individuals have been identified as Craig Larkin and Justin Harris. The police say what's disturbing

is that the gunmen were firing high powered assault weapons indiscriminately in an area where young kids normally play. Just in are the pictures of the three men involved in today's deadly confrontation. The police are urging anyone with information to call the police where you'll remain anonymous and may be eligible for a reward. This is still an active crime scene and as we learn more, we'll keep our viewers informed. I'm Michael Criswell, back to you, Lisa."

"Damn, that's Craig from the apartments, ain't it?"

"Yeah, and that's that nigga Blue who be with him."

"I've seen him but I don't know him. Tamaya gon trip when she hears about Craig."

"Why, she used to holla at him?"

"Not really, I mean he used to give her money and you know how that go."

"Mmm hmm! And what, you used to holla at his partner?"

"Boy, didn't I just tell you that I don't know him personally."

"Yeah, I hear you."

"Alright, now, don't start trippin."

"Look, I'm gon go next door to see if Curt saw the new—."

"Hold up, cause I'm coming with you," Crystal replied while jumping off the bed and after slipping on a pair of shoes, she followed Curt to the door. After walking out of the room, they went next door and knocked several times. Seconds later, Tamaya opened it.

“Hey, y’all seen the news?” Crystal asked before easing past her, and after letting Curt in, Tamaya closed the door behind him.

“You talking about the shit in the apartments with Craig?”

“Yeah, we just watched it.”

“Damn, that’s fucked up.”

“Yea, but who was the other nigga?”

“Oh, that’s Trigga. He’s the nigga who be robbing from the Diamonds.”

“Yeah, well, he picked the right ones cause that nigga Blue ain’t fuckin off. Remember them niggas that got shot up in the McDonald’s drive thru on 54th Street and 7th Avenue a couple months ago?”

“Yeah, what about ‘em?”

“They say he’s the one who did that.”

“Yeah, well, fuckin with City of Miami Police, both of ‘em came up short.”

“True, but they went out like soldiers.”

“Yeah, but I ain’t tryin to go out like that,” Snag said.

“Man, what’s gon be gon be and ain’t nothing we can do about it. We played big boy games, so we gotta play by big boy rules, it’s that simple.”

“Maybe for you, but I’m trying to be smarter than that.”

“Yeah, I hear you, but anyway, I’m going back next door to get some rest, you coming?”

“In a minute,” Tamaya replied as he headed for the door.

“Yeah, well, just knock and I’ll open the door for you,” Curt said before walking out. As the door closed, all she could say to herself was that she’s tried.

***

"Hey, detective!"

"Yeah, what you got?"

"Well, you ain't gon believe this, but you remember the shooting that happened the other night on 111th Street and 7th Avenue?"

"Yeah, what about it?"

"Well, the gun found on one of the shooters has been linked to it. You know what else?"

"No, what?"

"There was another shooting recently on 101st Street between 7th and 8th Avenue. The gun used in that crime was also found inside the apartment along with over fifty thousand dollars."

"So, what you're saying is that our shooters may have been involved in two other shootings?"

"Murders actually because both victims are deceased, and according to the ballistics report, both guns are the weapons that were used in those crimes."

"Alright, and the other dead guy is linked to a murder in Opa-Locka?"

"That's right."

"So, what the fuck's going on? I mean, on one hand, we've got two guys who were possibly responsible for two murders. On the other hand, I've got one guy who's a suspect or at least was in another one, and now, we've got three dead guys who can't tell us shit. Then, on top of that, we still don't know why they were trying to kill each other."

"Well, they definitely had their reasons because from

what we witnessed, it seems as if they were waiting for him. As soon as this car pulled in the parking lot, the one who was sitting in the car used it to block the front gate. Then, as the car went around the side of the building, the other one opened fire on him."

"Yeah, and that's when the first one we saw joined in."

"Okay, but it all comes back to one thing. Why did they want him dead? I mean, obviously the guy in the car came around here expecting trouble because he had an AK-47 with two fully loaded sixty round clips on the front seat with him."

"Well, whatever the reason, we'd better figure out something because the lieutenant will be here soon and trust me, he's gonna want some answers."

"Yeah, tell me about it," Detective Nelson replied. And as he went about trying to find them, he thought about Tamaya Taylor and the bank robbers who were still out there.

CHAPTER 52

"So, what's up, you ready to do this?" Curt asked while pulling up in the banks parking lot.

"Yeah, but I'll be lying if I said I wasn't nervous," Tamaya replied.

"All you gotta do is remember what we practiced and you'll be alright. Now listen, I'm gon leave the car running when we go in. That way, when we come out, all you gotta do is put in in gear and smash the gas."

"Oh, so I'm driving when we come out?"

"Yeah, so when you see me heading for the door, just start making your way to the car. Now, the first thing I'm gon do is deal with the security guard by the door while you make sure everybody gets on the floor, you got it?"

"Yeah, I got it."

"Alright, then let's go handle our business," Curt said while chambering a round in his AK and pulling the ski mask down over his face.

Quickly following his lead, Tamaya pulled the ski mask

down over her face before chambering a round in the AK she carried. Then, after watching him climb out the car and head for the double doors, she followed close on his heels.

With her heart pounding in her chest, Tamaya gripped the AK tightly. While carefully scanning the area and spotting no one, they rushed through the doors catching everybody by surprise.

"Everybody on the ma'fucking floor!" Curt screamed while leveling his gun at the security guard, and after removing his gun and radio, he ordered him to the floor.

"Alright, everybody listen up. Nobody has to get hurt, but if y'all don't cooperate, that's exactly what's gon happen. This ain't y'all money so if you're thinking about being a hero, think again. Your money is insured so you're gonna get it regardless. In the meantime, just keep your heads down and we'll be out of here before you know it. How much time we got left?"

"Eighty seconds," Tamaya replied.

"Alright, ladies, y'all know the drill," he said while walking towards the teller stations. "And if anybody puts a dye pack in this bag, I'll kill every one of you, do you understand?"

Meanwhile, keeping an eye on the customers sprawled out on the floor Tamaya, spotted the security guard acting suspiciously. Suddenly realizing that he was reaching for something tucked in his pants, she panicked. Having already made up her mind that she wasn't going to jail, she leveled her gun in his direction and the minute she saw the small gun, she fired. The sound was deafening, catching everybody by surprise, and suddenly turning to see what had happened, Curt saw the security guard blood pouring from his body.

"What the fuck did you do?" Curt screamed.

"He was going for a gun."

"Yeah, but you ain't supposed to shoot nobody."

"Well, what was I supposed to do?"

"Look, just relax alright," Curt said while reaching down to grab the bag of money and while heading for the door, he scooped up the gun on the way by.

"Go! Go! Go!" He screamed as Tamaya burst through the door, and after rushing outside, they hurried to the car before jumping in. Quickly putting the car in gear, she backed out of the parking space and sped out of the parking lot.

"Which way?" she asked excitedly.

"Go left to the Flat Tops," Curt looked out the back window to make sure they weren't being followed. Minutes later, they pulled into the parking lot of the Flat Tops, and quickly spotting the Charger, she pulled in next to it.

After scanning the area carefully, they got out the car before climbing into the Charger, starting it up, and driving off.

"Alright, now what?"

"Go back the way we came."

"Why?"

"Cause I want to see what they're doing. Plus, we gon change cars again."

"Alright," Tamaya said as they approached the bank, and as expected, the area was swarming with police.

"Damn, I can't believe you shot the security guard."

"Well, you told me to make sure nobody tried something,

right?"

"Yeah."

"Well, that's what I did. I mean, he had another gun so what was I supposed to do, wait for him to start shooting?"

"Nah, you did good. I'm just surprised, that's all," he said. Minutes later, they were pulling into the parking lot of Clown City. After parking next to the Camaro, Curt jumped out of the car. Quickly shutting if off, Tamaya followed him out. Climbing behind the wheel of the Camaro, Tamaya started it up, put it in gear, and as soon as Curt closed the door behind him, she sped off.

Meanwhile, as she eased into traffic, neither one of them paid attention to the car following them three cars back.

***

"See, that's what I'm talkin bout!" Snag screamed after storming back into the room.

"What's wrong?"

"I just told them that them crackas had Tamaya's face all over the damn TV and they still out there riding round like it's alright. They gon fuck round and get us all fucked up doing that stupid shit. All somebody gotta do is recognize her from the TV and it's a wrap."

"So, what you want to do? I mean, you already see he don't want to listen."

"Yeah, but at the same time, I don't want to just up and leave him cause then what he gon do?"

"Who cares! You need to be worrying about you. I mean, he don't care about nobody."

"Look, let me try to holla at him one last time when he gets back. If he don't listen, then at least I can say that I tried."

"Snag, listen to me. I ain't trying to go to jail and I don't want to see you go either, but if you keep waiting round for Curt, that's exactly what's gon happen. Now, I know he's your friend, but baby you've got to look out for yourself."

"Trust me, I hear you but we go too far back for me to just say fuck him."

"Well, let me ask you this, do you think he feels the same way? Cause he basically said fuck you, me, and everybody else before he left."

"Yeah, but he gets like that sometimes. Look, I understand what you're saying and if you want to leave, I'll respect it, but I've got to at least try to talk to him one last time."

"Yeah, alright, but in the meantime—hey look!" she suddenly pointing to the TV

"What?"

"It's says something about a bank robbery."

"Well, turn it up," Snag replied and after watching her do just that, he listened as the reporter spoke.

> "We interrupt regularly scheduled programming to bring you breaking news. Less than thirty minutes ago, the Bank of America located on 54th Street and 27th Avenue was robbed by a man and a woman wearing ski masks and carrying automatic weapons. It is reported that a security guard was killed, and right now, a massive man hunt is underway for the suspects. They

were last seen driving away in an all-black Nissan Maxima. Anyone with information is urged to call the police. I'm Michael Criswell from Northwest Miami Dade County, back to you, Lisa."

In a state of shock, they both stood there staring at the screen, and suddenly turning to look at each other, no words were needed because they both already knew.

CHAPTER 53

"So, let me get this straight. You mean to tell me that you stood by and let this happen?" The lieutenant asked while standing with Detective Nelson and Officer Chambers in the parking lot of the Silver Blue Lakes Apartment complex.

"Well, sir, it wasn't exactly like that."

"Wait a minute! Did you not see one of the shooter's cars blocking the entrance before exiting the vehicle with the AK?"

"Yes, sir."

"And did you not witness the victim enter the complex for the second time?"

"Yes, sir."

"Yet you did nothing to stop him?"

"Sir, we were conducting surveillance on a possible suspect in the deaths of two police officers during a bank robbery. We initially didn't want to blow our cover, but when the shooting started, we really had no other choice."

"Detective, do you understand what a public relations nightmare this is going to be? People are having rallies because of the senseless violence and you allowed two men with automatic weapons to open fire on a car in an area that's usually crowded with kids because you didn't want to blow your cover? Is that what you expect me to tell the commissioner?"

"Well, you could tell him that along with three bad guys being taken off the streets, three other murders have been solved."

"You're real funny, you know that detective? But let me explain something to you. We all have sworn to protect and serve the public and I take that very seriously. When the shit hits the fan, you're gonna be knee deep in it, so I suggest you get ready. Do you understand?"

"Yes sir."

"Good, now have your report on my desk by seventeen hundred hours."

"You'll have it," Detective Nelson replied before watching the lieutenant turn and walk away. The minute he was out of earshot, Detective Nelson turned to Officer Chambers.

"I wish I could just punch him in his damn mouth."

"Yeah, so does half the department."

"Only half."

"Well, some of 'em wouldn't have the heart to even if they allowed it."

"Well, I would, and trust me, I'd try to break my hand doing it," Officer Chambers replied.

"Alright, so now what? She'd have to be crazy to show up round here now."

"Maybe, but I've met some that'll test the odds."

"I'm sure you have, but remember, we've still got two cop killers out there."

"Yeah, don't remind me. Matter of fact—" and before he could finish his sentence, he was interrupted by the sound of his phone ringing.

"Shit, what now?" he said while pulling it out and flipping it open. "Hello! When? Where? Anybody hurt? You're kidding. Alright, well listen, nobody goes in or comes out til I get there, do you understand? Good, and Mike, we end this today. Okay, bye."

"What's going on?" Officer Chambers asked as soon as he hung up.

"Another bank was hit. Only this time, they made a mistake."

"How?"

"A good Samaritan followed them back to their hotel."

"You're kidding."

"I don't kid, Officer Chambers. Now, a perimeter is being set up around the hotel as we speak, so let's go."

"Alright, but have they figured out how they're going to handle it?"

"That's open for discussion, but one thing's for sure."

"What?"

"It ends today. Now, come on."

***

"Damn, nigga, where the fuck y'all been?" Snag asked while eyeing his friend warily.

"None of your ma'fuckin business, and since when I gotta

answer to you?"

"Since you all of a sudden decided to rob a bank without me."

"Man, you trippin. Ain't nobody robbed no bank."

"Oh, no, then what's in the bag?"

"None of your fuckin business."

"That's the money from the bank, huh?

"Nigga, I told you ain't nobody robbed no bank."

"Oh, so that wasn't you and Tamaya on TV?"

"Huh."

"On TV, stupid ass nigga. Them crackas had y'all on the damn TV and I told you that you was gon get us all fucked up with that stupid shit."

"Man, fuck that, what I do is my ma'fucking business."

"Oh, so y'all did do it?"

"What if I did?"

"Then, you're a stupid ass nigga."

"Man, fuck you!"

"Nah, nigga fuck you cause I'm round here tryin to look out for you and you round here doing dumb shit. You know, you the only nigga I'd go all out for but doing that dumb shit you just did, you showed me that you don't give a fuck about nobody but yourself."

"Alright, so now what? Cause I really ain't tryin to hear that shit right now," Curt replied dryly.

"Alright, then you do you cause I'm through with you."

"Man, whatever," Curt said as Crystal and Snag headed for the door, and after watching them walk out, they bolted the door behind them.

"Damn, I can't believe they did that stupid shit. All the

ma'fuckin heat we got on us already and then they go do that dumb shit, that crazy."

"I tried to tell you," Crystal cut in.

"Yeah, you did, but now I see it for myself."

"Alright, so now what?"

"We out of here, that's what. If he wants to go to jail being stupid, that's on him."

"Okay, but where we going?"

"Away from here. We can figure out exactly where later."

"Alright, just give me a minute to get all my stuff picked up," Crystal said as she began gathering her things. She had no idea that they were about to receive the surprise of their lives.

***

"Alright, so what we got?" Detective Nelson asked while climbing out of his car at the staging area around the corner from the hotel.

"Well, about an hour ago, we received a call from a Mr. Santiago saying that he was pulling up in the parking lot of the Bank of America when two individuals ran out wearing ski masks and carrying machine guns. They jumped into a car and sped off, and he followed them to an apartment complex located on 53rd Street and 27th Avenue where they switched cars. Then, after leaving there, he followed them to another apartment complex located on 64th Street and 27th Avenue where they switched cars again. Finally, he followed them to the hotel and that's when he called us."

"Okay, but has any of this been confirmed?"

"Well, the stolen cars have been found exactly where he

said they'd be and they're being processed as we speak. The hotel room he pointed out is registered under the name of Crystal Bridges, and get this, she also rented the room next door."

"Okay, who's watching the hotel?"

"We've got people posted up on all sides. Anybody tries to leave, we're on 'em. We even got a man at the front desk."

"Alright, the first thing I want to do is to try to evacuate as many of the rooms as possible. These people are armed and extremely dangerous and I have no doubt that they'll shoot anybody who they see as a threat. I don't want innocent bystanders getting caught in the crossfire if it comes to that. Has SWAT been notified?"

"Yes, sir, they're in route and so is a negotiator."

"Well, I doubt they'll listen, but it's worth a shot."

"Anything's worth a shot if it'll avoid bloodshed," Officer Chambers replied.

"I agree, but some things are unavoidable," Detective Nelson shot back.

"Okay, what's the plan? All this talk about death is freaking me out."

"Why? I mean, we all gotta die sometime."

"Yeah, I just hope it's not today."

"Okay, people listen up," Detective Nelson said suddenly switching gears. "We've got four individuals holed up inside the hotel around the corner and they are armed and extremely dangerous. They are suspects in at least three bank robberies and they're also suspected of killing three people, two of them our own. We hope to take 'em, alive, but if we are fired on, I'm authorizing each of you to return fire. Is that understood?"

"Yes, sir," they all replied in unison.

"Good, now does anybody have any questions? Alright then, somebody give me a vest." He said while removing his jacket. After being handed one, he put it on while contemplating his next move. "Alright, let's go people, and hopefully they'll go quietly."

"And what if they don't?" Someone asked.

"Then we take 'em down by any means necessary."

CHAPTER 54

Trying her best to control her excitement, Tamaya stood off to the side while watching Curt count the pile of money in the middle of the bed. When he'd argued with Snag earlier, he'd wanted to say something so badly, but when Curt suddenly dumped the bag of money out on the bed, she focused her mind on more important matters.

"Damn!" Curt screamed while walking away from the bed.

"What's wrong?"

"We only got hundred and seventy grand."

"Well, that's good, ain't it?"

"It's alright, but I mean, we usually get over two hundred grand."

"So, what you think happened?"

"Shit, what I know happened," he replied. "When you shot that security guard, we had to leave sooner than we anticipated, so we don't hit all the teller stations."

"I'm sorry, but he was going for a gun."

"I know, and I'm not mad at you."

"You sure?" she asked almost pleadingly.

"Yeah, I'm sure. Now, come here," he said while reaching out to her. Taking her in his arms, he pulled her to him before kissing her passionately.

Suddenly reaching down to massage him through his pants, Tamaya fantasized about making love on a bed full of money, and realizing that this could be her only chance, she decided to go for it.

Breaking their embrace, she looked into his face unbuckling his pants, then after pushing them down around his ankles, she grabbed him and began massaging him back and forth. Rubbing her thumb across the head of his dick, she could sense his anticipation, and suddenly without a word, she got down on her knees in front of him and took him in her mouth. Sucking him slowly in and out of her mouth, Tamaya could feel herself becoming wetter by the minute, and wanting so badly to satisfy him, she suddenly increased her pace.

Knowing he wouldn't last long if she kept it up, Curt pulled her up and began undressing her. Then, after spreading the money out on the bed, he laid her down on top of it before climbing between her legs. Pushing them back farther, he rubbed his dick around the outside of her pussy, and while looking down at her lustfully, he buried himself insider of her.

***

"Alright, everybody, hold your positions," Detective

Nelson said while looking out over the men spread out across the parking lot. “The negotiator is five minutes out, so we’ll wait and give him a chance to talk to them before we make a decision to go in.”

“Okay, but what if—no, wait! I think I see somebody coming out of one of the rooms. Hey, that’s the other girl we saw on the bank’s surveillance tape.” Officer Chambers suddenly said.

“Are you sure?”

“I’m positive.”

“Alright, let ‘em drive out the lot.”

“What!”

“I said let ‘em drive out the lot. We can pick ‘em up down the street.”

“Why when we can do it right here?”

“Do you want a bloodbath out here?”

“No.”

“Then let’s do it my way,” Detective Nelson replied. “Right now, the people in the other room have no idea that we’re out here. If we try to take ‘em down now and they start shooting, what do you think will happen?”

“The two in the other room will know we’re out here.”

“Exactly, now let them leave and we’ll take em’ down the street.”

“Okay, but I sure hope you know what you’re doing.”

“Trust me on this,” Detective Nelson replied. “Now, I want some units on standby to take down that car. I’d prefer that they were taken alive, but if need be, do what you have to do. Damn, where’d that news truck come from?”

“They got a scanner now, so they picked up on radio

transmissions."

"Yeah, well try to keep 'em out of the way."

"Alright, I got you, but you think the suspects saw us?"

"I don't know, but I doubt it."

"Yeah, well, there they go," Officer Chambers said as the car drove out of the parking lot, and after watching it drive out of sight, they waited patiently.

"Everybody, stay focused, we've still got two people inside the hotel. Any sign that they know we're here?"

"That's a negative, but I've just been informed that they're stopping the first car now."

"Alright, keep me informed. Any word on the negotiator?"

"Not yet."

"Well, let me know as soon as he gets here," Detective Nelson said. As soon as the words left his mouth, they received confirmation.

"Hey, they're both being taken into custody now."

"No shots fired?"

"None."

"Good," and turning his attention back to the hotel, Detective Nelson mumbled softly to himself, *two down, two to go.*

***

Damn! Curt said to himself as Tamaya slipped up and down on his dick, and while pulling her down onto him, he pushed up into her. Suddenly changing positions, Tamaya turned around and grabbed his ankles, and with her voluptuous ass now facing him, she began bouncing up and down on him.

"Mmm, shit!" He screamed softly as she increased her pace and wanting him deeper inside of her, she slammed down on him with abandon.

Damn, this dick's good, she said to herself as he fucked her hard and fast. Loving the feeling of him deep inside of her, she threw her head back and moaned with pleasure.

Feeling the tension rising, she grinding her hips into him and as the wave of pleasure washed over her, she came while coating his dick with her juices.

Minutes later, she felt his body tense up and knew that he was on the verge of cumming and catching him by surprise, she climbed of him, turned around, and took him in her mouth.

"Ah, shit!" He screamed as she began sucking him in and out of her mouth. Clearly excited by her efforts to please him, he came, flooding her mouth with his seed. Continuing to suck him in and out of her mouth, Tamaya swallowed everything he had to offer, and just when he thought it couldn't get any better, she began deepthroating him over and over again. Suddenly, something on the TV caught his attention, causing him to sit up in the bed.

"Hey, ain't that the hotel?" He asked.

"Huh? What you talkin bout?"

"Right there on the TV. Ain't that the hotel?"

"Yeah, but what the fuck," Tamaya said while staring at the screen, and as the realization of what they were watching hit them, they both ran to the window and looked outside.

"Oh, shit!" Curt screamed after seeing all the police cars

downstairs.

"How did they find us?" Tamaya asked.

"It don't mater. You see all them ma'fuckers out there?"

"Yeah, I do."

"Well, we fucked," he replied before grabbing his pants and while stepping into them, he tried to weigh his options. Suddenly spotting a reporter on the screen, he walked over to the TV and turned it up.

> "We're live from the Days Inn Hotel where the police say that two people suspected of several bank robberies and the deaths of two police officers are hiding inside. Two more suspects have been arrested without incident. But due to the latest development, it's unclear how this will end. According to the police, the Bank of America located on 54th Street and 27th Avenue was robbed this morning and a security guard was killed as the robbers escaped. Due to the quick thinking of a concerned citizen, the suspects were followed to this hotel after switching cars twice. We'll be staying one the scene of this developing story and as we learn more, we'll keep the public informed. I'm Michael Criswell live in Miami-Dade County, back to you, Lisa."

"Damn, we got followed by a ma'fuckin' hero! Man, I don't believe this shit," Curt said while pacing back and forth.

"And how the fuck did Snag and Crystal get caught? I thought they were still in the room?

"They must've left?"

"Curt, I don't want to go to jail."

"Me either," he replied, and as soon as the words left his mouth, he knew how it would all end.

CHAPTER 55

"Where's the damn negotiator? He was supposed to be her fifteen minutes ago!" Detective Nelson screamed.

"I'm right here, sir," a small man with wire rimmed glass replied while approaching. "I apologize, but I got stuck in traffic."

"Yeah, yeah, tell it to somebody who cares. All I want to know is can you get them two people out of that room without anybody having to shed blood?"

"All I can do is try, but before I can even do that, I need to find out as much as I can about them."

"Well, I can't tell you much about the man because we don't even know who he is. The woman's name is Tamaya Taylor, age twenty four, and according to witness' accounts, she shot a security guard during the most recent back robbery."

"What are they armed with?"

"AK-47's, but what does that have to do with anything?"

"Well, according to research, the bigger the gun the more superior the suspect may feel."

"Is this theory based on some mumbo jumbo book shit?"

"No, it's based on facts. It is well know that a suspect carrying a high powered assault weapon will feel far superior than he would if he were carrying a six shooter. Research has also proved that someone carrying an assault weapon like the one you just described would be more inclined to use it in a standoff than he would if he were carrying the six shooter I just mentioned."

"I'm sure they would," Detective Nelson replied. "But I still want to know, can you take them out of the hotel room without it resorting to that?"

"As the old saying goes, nothing beats a failure but a try."

"Alright, then, here's what I need you to do. Get him on the phone and explain to them that there's only one way out of there. Tell them that their friends are already in custody and that it's in their best interests to come out peacefully so we can all go home."

"Detective, I'm quite capable of doing my job, so if you'd please hand me a phone and the number, I'll call and see what state of mind these individuals are in."

"Fair enough," Detective Nelson replied while handing the phone and number to him. As he along with Officer Chambers looked on, the man flipped open the phone and dialed the number.

***

"Who's that? Tamaya asked after being startled by the sound of the phone ringing.

"That's probably them ma'fuckers downstairs," Curt

replied.

"Who, the police?"

"Yeah, who else you think it is?"

"Well, what do you think they want?"

"Shit, how I'm supposed to know?"

"Curt, answer the phone."

"Man, I don't want to talk to them ma'fuckers."

"Look, just answer the phone, alright?"

"Yeah, alright, but man, I ain't trying to hear that bullshit they talking," he replied while grabbing the phone. "What! That ain't none of your business, who's this? Alright, then, Clarence check this out. If anybody comes to this door, he gets it. Nah, we ain't coming out, but you heard what I just said? Alright, but if you think I'm bullshittin, I'll show you better than I can tell you. What you mean, what we want? We want y'all to leave us the fuck alone. Now, how you gon tell me you can't do that? Y'all the police and y'all can do what the fuck y'all want to do. Well, I tell you what, we ain't coming out and like I said, if a ma'fucker comes to the door, he getting it. Yeah, I hear you," Curt said before slamming the phone down and suddenly reflecting on the situation they were in, he grabbed the phone and slung it across the room.

"So, what did they say?" Tamaya asked nervously.

"They want us to come out and give ourselves up. Talkin bout they don't want nobody to get hurt."

"Well, what are we gonna do?"

"I know I ain't tryin to go to jail."

"Me either, but at the same time, we can't stay here."

"No, but you see all them ma'fuckin police out there?"

"Yeah, I see 'em, but either we have to go out or they

coming in."

"Yeah, and you know what that means right?"

"Nah, what?"

"That nine times out of ten, we might not make it out of here alive." Curt replied.

"Well, it was a good ride while it lasted," Tamaya said tryin to put on a brave face.

"True, but it was supposed to last longer than that."

"Hey, shit happens, you know. I mean, hind sight is always a ma'fucker."

"Yeah, I know," Curt replied while contemplating their next move. Suddenly thinking about the inevitable end, he grabbed the AK from the side of the bed and chambered a round.

***

"Alright, people look alive!" Detective Nelson screamed as everybody began scrambling to get into position.

"We gave them a chance, and it they don't come out within the next fifteen minutes, we're going in. Where's the SWAT commander?"

"I'm right here, detective."

"Okay, I want a man on these two buildings right there. Can you do that?"

"Of course, anything else?"

"No, that's it for now. Once they get in position, they should have a clear line of sight to the suspect's room. Chambers?"

"Yes, sir."

"Take three men with you and get into position by the stairs. That way, you'll have a clear view of them if they decide to exit the room."

"I'm on it," Officer Chambers replied before storming off. Suddenly left to his own thoughts, Detective Nelson reflected back on the many cases he'd worked over the years. Although tedious and time consuming, he'd closed them all and the one thing that all the suspects had in common, was that they didn't know when to stop.

"Hey, something's happening," somebody said interrupting his thoughts.

"What's going on?"

"I'm not sure, but somebody opened the door."

"Do you know who it was? I mean, was it him or her?"

"I don't know."

"Okay, people we might be getting ready," and before he could finish his sentence, Curt and Tamaya burst out of the room firing their AK's indiscriminately at the officers in the parking lot.

Caught off guard momentarily by their brashness, the police dove for cover as the high velocity rounds pierced metal and shattered glass. Then, almost seemingly in unison, they all quickly recovered and returned fire.

Curt and Tamaya didn't stand a chance as round after round tore into their bodies. Running on pure adrenaline, Curt continued firing.

Hit several times in her chest, neck, and face Tamaya was slammed back against the wall. Suddenly dead on her feet, she pitched forward over the railing before landing on the pavement below.

Feeling his life slipping away, Curt tired his best to stay focused, but after losing so much blood, there was little he could do. Falling to his knees, he tried desperately to stand, but as the police kept firing, he knew it was a lost cause.

Lying face down on the concrete, Curt reflected on the events that led up to this moment. Right before taking his last breath, he realized that he'd gotten caught up like so many others before him chasin' paper.

THE END!

A Sneak Preview of upcoming books by Circle Six Publishing

Coming Soon

Tricked

Chapter 1

With her nerves on edge Sheyenne sat quietly as Calvin drove out of the parking lot and made a left on 27th Avenue. After making a quick right on 183rd Street he drove towards his house in Miami Lakes.

Meanwhile, in the backseat Eureka admired the trucks plush interior while eying the man driving. She as initially intimidated by his size, but after thumbing the safety off the gun she carried in her purse she now focused on what lay ahead.

"So what's up, y'all good? Calvin asked suddenly while pulling up to the light on 183rd Street and 32nd Avenue.

"I am," Sheyenne replied while desperately trying to keep her nerves in check.

"What about you?" he asked while eyeing Eureka in the rearview mirror.

"Oh, I'm good," she shot back matter of factly.

"Alright then, so what's y'all names?

"I'm China Doll and my friends name is Sporty Black," Sheyenne replied while turning to face him.

"China Doll and Sporty Black, huh?"

"Yeah, now what's yours?"

"Calvin."

"And that's what people call you?"

"Yeah, why?

"No reason, I just thought they might've called you something else. Anyway where we goin?"

"To my house in Miami Lakes, why?"

"Just asking that's all."

"Yeah, well, I just hope it don't be no bullshit when we get to the house."

"No bullshit like what?"

"You know, where y'all start trippin."

"Well, if you payin like you weighin then we stayin," Eureka replied from the backseat.

"That ain't no problem."

"Well, it ain't gon be no bullshit," Eureka shot back.

Trying hard to contain his excitement Calvin couldn't wait to get home, and as soon as the light turned green he stepped on the gas. The truck shot forward, and as the sounds of push it by Rick Ross came blasting out of the speakers he weaved in and out of traffic barely avoiding another truck while making a left on 67th Avenue.

Minutes later he was pulling up in the yard of a two story brick home with a neatly manicured lawn. After pulling inside the garage they all got out and headed inside.

"Y'all make yourselves comfortable," he said before walking out of the room and as soon as he was gone Sheyenne turned to Eureka.

"So how we gon do this?" She asked nervously.

"If it was up to me I'd just shoot him and be done wit it," Eureka replied.

"Yeah, but then what we gon do?"

“We find his stash and get gone, that’s what.”

“Alright well listen,” and before she could say another word Calvin came back wearing nothing but a robe.

“Y’all want something to drink?”

“What you got?”

“Whateva y’all want.”

“Alright then, give us some patron on ice no chaser,” Sheyenne said in an attempt to stall.

“Comin right up.”

“Girl what you doin?” Eureka asked as soon as he walked off.

“What you mean?”

“What I mean is we don’t need to be getttin drunk.”

“We ain’t gettin drunk, we just.”

“Here you go,” Calvin suddenly said cutting him off.

After handing them their drinks he stepped back while looking them up and down. “So y’all want to chill down here or y’all want to go upstairs?”

Might as well go upstairs,” Eureka replied.

“Alright,” he said before heading for the stairs and as he began to climb the stairs the girls followed close behind.

Finally reaching the top of the stairs they proceeded to walk down the hall before suddenly stepping into a room you’d expect to see on the lifestyle of the rich and famous. Genuinely impressed the girls admired the marble floors and the king size four post bed, and suddenly eager to get it over with Eureka downed her drank before she began undressing.

Following her lead Sheyenne also began undressing and transfixed by her voluptuous breasts and neatly shaved pussy Calvin disrobed and climbed into bed.

Suddenly without a word Eureka grabbed her .380 Baretta out of her purse and pointed it at him.

"And what the fuck you gon wit that?" He asked with a smirk.

"You get off that bed and I'm goin show you," Eureka replied. "Now hand me that chain and watch you got on."

"Oh, so y'all tricks think y'all just gon come up in here and rob me like it's alright?"

"Look, just give us the chain and watch and we out of here." Eureka said.

"Then what? I mean y'all really think it's gon be that easy?"

"It is so far."

"Oh, yeah, well what if I just say fuck it and don't give y'all shit?"

"Then I'll bust a cap in your fat ass." Sheyenne said before raising her Sig Saur 9mm and pointing it at him.

"I don't believe this shit, I'm getting robbed by some tricks," he said in disbelief, and without warning Sheyenne fired hitting him in the leg.

"Ahh shit!" He screamed.

"I got your attention now, huh? Now take off that damn watch and chain."

"Alright but I hope y'all know that y'all done fucked up."

"Yeah, whateva, now don't make me ask you again."

"Alright here," he said while removing the watch and chain.

Looking up at her in disgust he threw them at her feet. Watching him warily Sheyenne bent down to pick up the jewelry.

"Now what?" Sheyenne asked while looking at her friend.

"Yeah, now what?" Calvin asked sarcastically.

"Shut up!" Eureka replied while contemplating her next move and seconds later it hit her. "So how does it feel to get tricked?" She asked with a smirk.

"What?"

"You heard me. Earlier you called us tricks now how does it feel to get tricked?"

"Y'all bitches gon pay for this."

"Maybe, but right now we got the upper hand, now say it."

"Say what?"

"That you got tricked."

"Man, y'all bitches crazy."

"I said say it," Eureka shot back and without another word Sheyenne hit I'm in the head with her gun.

Paint shot through him as he grabbed the side of his head and while looking up at her with hatred in his eyes all he could think about was getting out alive.

"Now say it," she said thought crunched teeth.

"Alright! Alright! Chill," he replied while trying to regain his composure.

"I ain't gon tell you again."

"Alright, I got tricked, you happy now?"

"Nah, ma'fucka now say it again."

"Look."

"Ma'fucker you heard what she said," Sheyenne suddenly cut in. "Now say it."

"Alright! Alright! I got tricked."

"You damn right," Eureka replied and without another

word she pulled the trigger.

“Oh, shit!” Sheyenne screamed as she watched Calvin slump back on the bed.

Covered in blood she stood wide eyed staring at Eureka.

“Look, don’t stand there help me search this ma’fucka,” Eureka said while dressing.

“Girl I’m covered in blood.”

“Well, go jump in the shower but hurry up so we can get out of here.”

“Alright,” Sheyenne replied before rushing into the bathroom.

Meanwhile, Eureka began searching and after pouring out the contents of the dresser drawers and coming up empty she made her way over to the closet. Snatching it open she began her search, and suddenly spotting a duffel bag in the back she snatched it up while trying to contain her excitement. Exiting the closet she placed the bag on top of the dresser, then after unzipping it she looked inside to see more money than she’d ever seen in her life. Stacks of money bound by rubber bands stared back at her. And grabbing one of the stacks she thumbed through it noticing nothing but big face hundreds.

“Jackpot!” she said to herself before dropping the money back in the bag and after zipping it closed she sat it on the floor before continuing her search.

“Found anything yet?” Sheyenne asked while comin into the room.

“Yeah, in the bag on the floor.” Eureka replied.

“What is it, money?”

“Yeah.”

"How much?"

"Look, we can count it later. Right now help me search this ma'fucka so we can get out of here."

"Alright," Sheyenne said before rushing off.

With renewed vigor Eureka tore through the closet like a woman possessed searching clothes and boxes before comin up empty. Then almost an afterthought she walked over to the bed and looked under it. Noticing a black briefcase she reached out and grabbed it before quietly rushing over to the dresser. Throwing the briefcase on top of it she suddenly realized that she needed a combination to open it.

"Damn!" she said in frustration and not wanting to miss an opportunity she decided to take it with them.

"Girl I ain't find nothing in the other rooms," Sheyenne said after suddenly rushing back into the room.

"Don't worry bout it, let's get out of here." Eureka replied before grabbing both the briefcase and duffel bag then rushing out the door.

"You gon call Denise?"

Nah, we'll leave in his truck then we'll call 'em to meet us somewhere."

"Alright, but don't you think we need to wipe everything down? You know to get rid of our fingerprints."

"Oh, shit! I ain't think about that," Eureka said as they finally made it out to the garage.

Suddenly spotting a gas can in the corner she quickly formulated a plan.

"Wait for me in the truck," she said before handing Sheyenne the duffel bag and briefcase.

After rushing over and grabbing the gas can she headed

back inside the house. Moments later she came running back into the garage, and after quickly climbing inside the waiting truck, Sheyenne backed out of the garage and sped off into the night.

Coming Soon

SNITCH

Prologue

"Fifth Ward is the spot where niggas get shot/ ho's ell cock and every block is hot/ niggas start shit but they don't want it wit Bill/'cause them ma'fucker know that blood gon spill/ever since I was a kid growin up in the bottom/I beat a niggas ass if I didn't I shot him/never gave a fuck about his family cryin/bottom line better his than mine/you come around wit that lie shit I kill it fast/throw a search party for your stinkin ass nigga/cause it's a motherfuckin rep thing/you got a set of nuts you better let them motherfuckers hang/even if you're facing twenty years you never rat/you do your time and you come on back/and if your homie real he'll take care your people while you're gon and bless you when you come back home/do your time and don't whine that the motherfuckin anthem/that's the type of shit most niggas can't fathom/them niggas tongues come unfurled/but that what separates the ghetto boys from girls. "

"Nigga, turn that shit down," Crack said before making a left on 174th Street and 43rd Avenue.

"Man, that's them Ghetto Boys," Wally replied while

turning down the volume.

"Yeah, yeah I hear you. But don't that nigga stay somewhere on this block?"

"Yeah, right down. Hold up! That's that nigga right there."

"Where."

"Right there," Wally said pointing as an all-black Chevy Impala drove past.

"Fuck!"

"Look, ain't no pressure. Just turn around."

"Man, I wanted to catch that nigga before he left the house."

"Yeah, but like I said ain't no pressure," Wally said while climbing into the backseat. "Just slide up on the side of his bitch ass and I got him."

Meanwhile, the driver of the black Impala was oblivious to the danger behind him. Suddenly changing lanes the drive slowed down before heading on the Palmetto Expressway.

"Damn, this nigga bout to get on the ma'fucking Expressway," Crack said in frustration.

"So what, just follow him."

"Yeah, but."

"Man, listen, how many times we done did this?"

"A bunch of times."

"Alright then stop trippin and let's handle our business."

Without replying Crack turned his attention back to the black Impala up ahead of them in traffic.

"Man, catch him before he gets to the Golden Glades Interchange," Wally said from the backseat.

"Nigga, chill, I got this," Crack replied before speeding

up.

While switching lanes Crack checked his rearview mirror for any signs of anything out of the ordinary, and quickly approaching the Golden Glade Interchange he zeroed in on the man driving the all-black Chevy Impala. Slowly gaining ground he waited patiently for an SUV to pass before sliding in behind it. Then with eyes locked in on the car ahead he began creeping into position.

"Get ready," Crack said just loud enough for his friend to hear.

"I been ready," Wally replied while positioning himself in the backseat.

Seconds later Crack eased his car up alongside the black Impala without trying to draw attention to himself. Suddenly stealing a glance at the car next to them he spotted a small child strapped in the backseat. And just as the opened his mouth to say something his friend opened fire.

CHAPTER 1

It was a Monday morning and inside the Miami Dade County Courthouse the mood was somber. Seated next to his lawyer Ricky Taylor A.K.A. Black Rick observed the bustle of activity going on around him. To his left, the States Prosecutor Amy Ryan and her associate Charles White sat discussing their trial strategy. Straight ahead sat the County Clerk a pretty redbone who stole glances at him occasionally while sorting files. The bailiff stood by the door as spectators and supporters entered and took their seats. Dressed in an all-black Armani suit with matching black gators Rick had been incarcerated without bail for two years for the crime of first degree murder, extortion and attempted first degree murder and with an arrogant smug he welcomed his day in court.

"Look at him, he thinks he's untouchable," the prosecutor said with a contempt.

"No matter cause when the trials over we'll wipe that smug right off his face, her partner replied.

Suddenly the bailiff announced "all rise" as the judge entered the courtroom and took his seat behind the bench.

"Judge Alex Rivera residing, you all may now be seated," the Bailiff continued.

"Thank you Robert," the judge replied. "Now what do we have this morning?"

"Good morning your honor. I'm Amy Ryan and my co-chair is Charles White for the state," the prosecutor said while approaching the bench.

"And I'm Steven Shaw, attorney for the defendant your honor."

"Okay, somebody give me an update on what we're doing here this morning."

"Your honor we have Ricky Taylor case number 19-90748, and he's charged with one count of first degree murder, extortion and attempted first degree murder," the court clerk replied.

"That is correct your honor, and his case has been set for trial this morning," the prosecutor added.

"Are all parties ready?"

"We are your honor," the defense attorney replied.

"So is the State your honor, but I have one small request?"

"Which is?" The judge asked while looking down at her over the rim of his glasses.

"Well, your honor, the state's main witness called earlier and it appears he'll be running a little late. If it is possible I'd like to ask you to delay.

"Delay!" the defense attorney screamed cutting her off. "Your honor, my client has been sitting in jail for two years and now that he has he day in court which I might add is his right, she wants to ask for a delay."

"First of all, in no way is asking for a one or two hour delay an infringement on your client's rights," the prosecutor replied. "And secondly, if your client had any regards for the victims' rights in this case we wouldn't be here now would we counselor?" she added sarcastically.

"Okay, you two," the judge interrupted, "Save the argument for the trial. Meanwhile, why wasn't the court notified of this before now?"

"Well, you honor, we were just recently notified that he had to drop his son off to daycare, and after that he'd be here."

"Ms. Ryan isn't it the states responsibility to make sure all of your witnesses are here on time?" The judge asked sternly.

"Yes your honor."

"Well, I'm granting you thirty minutes and if your witness is not here you'll proceed without him."

"But your honor, without him we have no case," The prosecutor said almost pleadingly.

"Then you should've had him detained as a material witness. That way there wouldn't have been a question of him being on time would it?"

"No sir."

"Good, now like I said in thirty minutes."

"Suddenly a flurry of activity interrupted him and as he looked on a police officer along with another woman approached the prosecutors table.

"Somebody want to tell me what's going on?" The judge asked clearly irritated by the interruption. "And who are these people?"

"Your honor, I'm Sandra Cowart and I'm an investigator for the State Attorney's office. With me is Detective Juan Leiva of the Miami Dade Police Department."

"Okay, and what is so important that you found it necessary to barge in here an interrupt these proceedings?"

"Well, your honor, about an hour ago there was a shooting involving a small child. Fortunately the child was uninjured but the same can't be said about the child's father."

"Okay, but what's that got to do with you barging in here?"

"Well, while the victim was being transported to Jackson Memorial Ryder Trauma Center, State Attorney Amy Ryans card was found in his pocket."

"Yes your honor, and unfortunately that victim was our primary witness in the case against Ricky Taylor," the prosecutor chimed in.

"Which means what exactly?" the judge asked while eyeing her over his glasses.

"Which mean that we have no case against the defendant your honor," the prosecutor said reluctantly.

"Your honor would you mind telling me what's going on?" Attorney Steven Shaw suddenly asked while approaching the bench.

"Well, counselor it seems that we have an unfortunate turn of events. According to this investigator the state's main witness was killed this morning, and that in turn jeopardizes the case against your client."

"What exactly do you mean it jeopardizes the case against

my client?" The attorney asked while trying to maintain his building excitement.

"What he's saying is that we may have to nol-pros all charges and reserve the right to recharge him if or when new evidence is found." The State's Attorney chimed in.

"Why, what happened or did you just realize you couldn't win?" Ricks attorney asked dryly.

"Let's just say that due to the extenuating circumstances it's the best course of action available," the judge replied. "On another note we have to get this on record so let's wrap this up."

"Your honor, if it's ok with the court I'd like to confer with my client about what's going on," Attorney Shaw cut in.

"You have five minutes counselor."

"It shouldn't take that long your honor."

Heading back over to the defense table he took his seat next to Rick.

"You're not going to believe what just happened," the said while leaving in closer.

"What?" Rick asked curiously.

"They have to drop the charges."

"Say what!" Rick screamed.

"Hey! Hey! Not so loud," his attorney said. "It seems their main witness was killed this morning on the way here and without him they have no case."

"Is that right," Rick stated as a sly smile came across his face.

"Yeah, that's."

"Counselor are you ready?" The judge suddenly asked

cutting him off.

"Yes your honor we are."

"Okay, well can you and your client approach the bench? We need to get this done."

"No problem your honor."

With an air of arrogance Black Rick stood before approaching his attorney in front of the courtroom. After stopping next to him he looked over and winked at the court clerk before turning his attention to the man in the black robe.

"Young man today's your lucky day. Due to an unfortunate evert the state's going to have to dismiss all charges against you. But they will reserve the right to recharge you in the event that new evidence is found, do you understand?"

"Yeah, I understand," Black Rick replied with a smirk.

"Okay, well at this time the prosecutor will announce it for the record."

"In the State of Florida in and for Miami Dade County we the State's Attorney's Office well nol-pro case number 19-90748 against Ricky Taylor. We will reserve the right to recharge him at a later date in the event that new evidence arises," the prosecutor said.

"You find something funny?" The judge asked suddenly while looking down at Rick over the rim of his glasses.

"What it's a crime to smile?" Rick snapped back.

"No, but this is a very serious matter and you need to take it seriously."

"Yeah, and I have also been locked up for the past two years. Now can I go?" Rick asked arrogantly.

"Yeah, you can, but you'd better hope to God they don't find the evident to bring you back before me?"

"Or what? Rick asked challengely.

"Your honor, please excuse my client," attorney Shaw cut in. "After two years of being incarcerated he's just ready to home to his family."

"Yeah, well let me tell you something young man. I don't believe in coincidences and its might strange that on the morning of your trail the state's main witness is killed. I suggest you do something with your attitude or you could find yourself in more trouble than you're prepared to deal with, are we clear?"

"Yeah, we clear?" Rick stated dryly.

"Good, now you're free to go. This court is adjourned."

Coming Soon

“TAKING NO SHORTS’ 4
(FRENCHIES RETURN)

Excerpt from Book 3

After leaving the hotel Frenchie had Frog call everybody to tell them to meet him at the warehouse. Upon arriving themselves Frenchie parked and went inside. Seeing everybody else already there he immediately go down to business.

“Alright everybody listen up. Remember I told y’all that after tonight we might have to go away for a while. Well, we can’t wait til after tonight.”

“Wait a minute! What’s going on?”

“We’ve got to leave tonight, cause if we don’t by this time tomorrow we’ll either be dead or in jail.”

“So what we gon do, just pack up and leave?” Latrice screamed.

“Ain’t gon be no packin’. If we go, we go straight from here cause if I know Detective Diaz like I know him he’s rounding up everybody he can get so I wouldn’t be surprised if they came tonight.”

Damn! But what about our money all the rest of our stuff?”

“I’ve called and made arrangements to have all our

money transferred to offshore accounts. We'll still have access to our money and it'll be untraceable. I've also agreed to sell the construction company and salons to Miguel and Papa Zoe for $10 million, with just the $20 million dollar contract for the Marlins Stadium getting our money won't be a problem."

"What about all the dope we got stashed in storage?"

"Miguel and Papa Zoe have also agreed to take care of it and once it's sold we're to receive $10.5 million dollars."

"So in other words, we have no reason to stay here."

"Well, I ain't leaving," Latrell suddenly said. "I can't just leave, who gon look out for Fats?"

"You."

"What?"

"I said you gon look out for him cause he's coming with us." Frenchie replied. "Besides, where we going he'll be able to get all the rest he needs."

"So where we going?"

"Trust me you're gonna love it. Now there's a private jet siting at Opa-Locka Airport gassed up and ready to go."

"So let's go. What are we waiting for?" Frog stated. As everyone began walking to their cars Big D walked over to Frenchie.

"Hey man!"

"Yeah, what's up?"

"You still thinking bout going after them ma'fuckas in Chicago?"

"It's being taken care of, and don't worry we won't ever have to deal with them again."

***

Back at Frenchie's house, Detective Diaz stood out in front with members of A.T.F., the F.B.I. and the local police department waiting for the signal to enter.

"Okay, people listen up," Agent Hawkins screamed. "We have personnel in position at each of the T.N.S. members houses, and just in case there's some shooting we also have police coverage within a two block radius around each of their homes."

"Officer Rogers!"

"Yeah,?"

"Get on the horn and tell everybody to be ready to hit 'em in two minutes, and I mean hit 'em hard. I don't want anybody coming in or out and leave no stone unturned. These people are armed and extremely dangerous, and if they resist do what you have to do. Under no circumstances are any of them to get away, is that understood?"

The minutes seemed to tick by slowly when suddenly they all heard the radio crackle and the familiar words "permission confirmed."

"Go! Go! Go!" Agent Hawkins screamed as the agents rushed forward throwing flash grenades through windows kicking in doors and fanny out inside with precision as they'd done countless times before.

"All clear," came over the radio indicating that the house was secured. Walking inside the house Detective Diaz heart sank when one of the agents said, "Nobody's here."

"What?"

"The house is empty detective. I mean, see for yourself."

As he began going from room to room he heard similar repeats coming from each of the other residences. Walking back outside Detective Diaz watched as the member of other agencies packed up their gear and began leaving. After watching the last car pull off Detective Diaz slumped against his car then looked up toward the sky "Frenchie where the fuck are you?"

Six Months Later

"Brian please hold the noise down or you'll wake the baby."

"Ah ma, but I want to play with her."

"You can play with her when she wakes up. Right now she's sleeping."

"Okay," Brian replied as he turned and ran out of the room.

"That boy," Chiqueta said. "I don't know what I'm gon do with him."

"Maybe we need to give him a little brother," Frenchie said with a smirk.

"You would say that wouldn't you?" She playfully replied.

"Hey, I'm just trying to help."

"Maybe, but we'll talk about that later."

"Fair enough, so what would you like to do today?"

"I don't know, how bout you?"

"I don't know either, but I'm sure we'll think of something."

"So have you heard from Raul?"

"No but Martha called."

"How's she doing?"

"Oh, she's fine. She told me to tell everybody hi."

"I miss Ole Martha."

"Yeah, me too," Frenchie replied. Grabbing the remote control and after turning on the TV Chiqueta took a seat next to him.

Suddenly a breaking news story caught their attention, and after tuning up the TV they both listened in silence as the reporter spoke.

> "We interrupt this regular scheduled program to bring you a story we're working on out of Chicago. The bodies of five mob bosses were found in their houses this morning. The police aren't saying much but sources tell us that the police are preparing for what could be one of the biggest mob wars in Chicago's history as the remaining families fight for control over territories left by these deaths."
>
> "Again the bodies of five mob bosses were found dead inside their homes, spurring rumors of an impending mob war, as soon as we learn more we'll notify viewers with more details. From Chicago, this is TV correspondent Mike Notion. Now back to our regular scheduled program."

"Did you have anything to do with that?"

"No, that was Raul's doing."

"So, it's over?"

"For now it is."

"When will we be able to go home, or will we ever?"

"That I don't know," Frenchie replied. "But I thought

you liked it here?"

"I do, but"

"But what?"

"I just never thought it would be home."

"Well, for now it is, so we might as well enjoy it."

What about the others?"

"What you mean?"

"I mean, what are they gonna say about our decision to stay here?"

"Actually they're the ones who suggested it and besides while Fats recovers it'll do a lot of good."

"That girl really loves him you know."

"Yeah, I know, and he's lucky to have her."

"Yeah, and I'm lucky to have you."

"You think so?"

"I know so Frenchie."

"So how bout we get married?"

"Wait, are you serious?"

"Yeah, I'm serious. We can have the wedding right here on the island."

"Oh, my God! There's so much to do," Chiqueta screamed, "But wait?"

"What's wrong?"

"Nothing, but what will the other's think?"

"Think about what?"

"You know us getting married."

"Chiqueta listen, you're family and besides it's my decision."

"Okay, but how would you feel about me asking the girls to be bridesmaids?"

"That'll be fine and I'm sure they'll be glad to."

"I hope so because I want this to be perfect."

It already is," Frenchie replied. "It already is."

CHAPTER 1
New Beginnings

Detective Diaz sat behind his desk deep in thought. Leaning back in his chair he looked around his office while reflecting back on his career that spanned twenty years and all the sacrifices he'd mad. After enduring two divorces he rarely spoke to or saw his children and any semblance of a normal life was a distant memory. Approaching sixty he was a proud man who prided himself on being able to outthink even the smartest criminals. However, he lay awake many nights thinking about Jamal Thomas A.K.A. Frenchie and his infamous T.N.S. crew. Five years ago to the day they'd simply vanished without a trace and now as he sat in his office pondering his impending retirement he wondered to himself if they'd ever be brought to justice.

While packing the last of his belongings he thought back to their last encounter and the vow he'd made and it ate at him that they'd that got away. Grabbing a stack of old files he put them in a box before loading them onto the cart with his personal belongings. After reluctantly taking one last look around his office he walked out into the hallway, and while contemplating the next chapter in his life he pushed his cart towards the record department. Starting over is a challenge for anyone but for someone nearing sixty it can be even harder. With much trepidation he signed the necessary paperwork before handing the clerk box of files and while thinking about a much needed vacation he headed outside to his car, climbed in and drove out of the parking lot.

***

Metropolitan Federal Correctional Facility
Chicago, Illinois

The prisoner's day starts early. The crackle of the intercom wakes him at 6:00am. The guards slip a tray with cold cereal and a plastic cup of watered down orange juice through the slot in his door of his cell. An eleven by nine cage in the special housing unit on the top floor of the federal facility in downtown Chicago where for the past five years he's spent twenty three hours a day.

The cell doesn't have a window but if it did he'd see the Chicago skyline. It's that close. He doesn't mind being in isolation away from the other prisoners because there were many who wanted him dead. Some for fear, others for revenge. Before his fall he was a powerful man who owned mansions, expensive cars, and gave orders to thousands of men. Now he has a blanket, two sheets, and a towel. Instead of custom made suits, he wears an orange jumpsuit, a white t-shirt and a pair of black crocs. He sits in a cage, eats garbage brought in on a tray.

Before his trial the prosecutor tried to get him to flip to become an informer but he refused. An informer is the lowest form of human life, a creature that does not deserve to live. He has his own code he would rather die or endure this kind of life then become such an animal.

He's fifty, the best case scenario extremely doubtful is that he gets thirty years. Even with credit for time served he'd be in his seventies before he walks out the door.

At 8:00 the guards start the morning count which takes about an hour. Then he's free until 10:30. For one hour a day the guards lead him handcuffed outside to a wired pen for recreation. Every third day he's taken for a shower. Occasionally he meets with his lawyer inside a tiny meeting room.

He' sitting in his cell filing out a commissary form. Ramen Noodles, Oatmeal Cookies, Coffee when the guard opens the door.

The guard shrugs, as the prisoner stands and presses his hand against the wall. As the guard shackles his ankles he's reminded of just how humiliating this was. Minutes later he's sitting across from his lawyer inside the tiny room.

"I received your message," the lawyer said skipping the formalities.

"And?"

"It's a death sentence for certain, a suicide pact."

"If I don't go through with it, I'm dead anyway so what's the difference?"

"The difference is that these types of things have always been pre-arranged with the other families to minimize the damage. What you're talking about is on another level altogether."

"Maybe it is, but I want you to tell them that if they agree with my terms I'll give them Frenchie."

"You're out of your mind, and as your lawyer I'd advise against it."

"Yes you are my lawyer and as your client I'm instructing you to make the deal. If you don't I'll fire you and hire someone who will," the prisoner replied sternly.

He couldn't tell him why this deal had to be made, couldn't tell him that delicate negotiations have been going on behind the scenes. He knew it was a risk, but it was a risk he had to take. If they kill him they kill him but he's not going to spend the rest of his life in a prison cell.

Without another word his lawyer stood to leave, and after watching him board the elevator the guard escorted him back to his cell where he'd wait for things to unfold.

ABOUT THE AUTHOR

Marlin Ousley is an author and the founder of Circle Six Publishing. A native of Miami. Florida, Marlin has the uncanny ability to capture the pulse of the streets with intelligence, strong character development and well thought storylines. He has a Bachelor's Degree in Business Management, and an Associate's Degree in Public Relations. His first novel Taking No Shorts a first of a trilogy has reach critical acclaim from critics and reader from around the country. He has three children, Lil Marlin, Anthony and Alexandra and he's hard at work on his next novel. Other books by Marlin Ousley; Taking No Shorts 1, 2 & 3, Corporate Thug parts 1 & 2.

Order Form

MAKE CHECKS AND MONEY ORDERS PAYABLE TO:

Circle Six Publishing
1245 N.W. 134th Street
Miami, Florida 33167
Mjousley50@aol.com or
circlesixpub@gmail.com

Name:____

Address:____

City:____________ State: ____________ Zip: ______________

Amount		Book Title or Pen Pal Number	Price
		Included for shipping for 1 book	**$4 U.S. / $9 Inter**

This book can also be purchased on:
AMAZON.COM/ BARNES&NOBLE.COM

Made in the USA
Middletown, DE
24 September 2021